SUGARING SEASON

STORIES FROM THORNTON & BEYOND

CAMERON D. GARRIEPY

CONTENTS

SUGARING SEASON

Cameron D. Garriepy

A Thornton Vermont Story

From the Earth to the Moon

ACKNOWLEDGMENTS

I am known to say that it takes a village to raise a novel—or in this case a short story—and I am pleased and grateful for the village in which I write.

My deepest thanks to Valerie Boersma for her priceless advice on mid-century American history and Americana, to Angela Amman and Mandy Dawson for a thorough and unflinching developmental edit, as well as their unwavering support and friendship, and to all of my readers for continuing to turn these pages.

As always, to my husband and son, to my parents and in-laws, thank you for putting up with my nonsense. You make this dream of mine possible and I love you.

I would be remiss if I did not offer up gratitude and an apology to Jules Verne for borrowing his rather famous title for this little tale.

"Wake up, son. This is your stop."

George Cartwright blinked at the elderly woman across the aisle of the coach car. Her crepey hand rested on his wrist.

"Port Henry, dear." She pointed out the window.

George peered at the slowing landscape. Six long years since he'd seen the particular color of the Adirondack sky. Six years since he'd smelled the wind off Lake Champlain. Six years of tracing the ridge line of the Green Mountains in his memory, letting his mind's eye drop just there—soaring into downtown Thornton and coming to rest on the front porch of the Gingerbread Victorian on Chapel Street that was his boyhood home.

When George was a child, he dreamed of spaceships as often as he dreamed of anything. In the summer of 1939, when his little brother reverently smoothed the edges of new *Superman* comics, ten-year-old George nudged them aside on the nightstand to make room for his grandfather's copy of Jules Verne's *From the Earth to the Moon*. Stars and infinite blue sang him a siren song. His red Elgin Robin became a sleek ship, his pumping legs rockets, flying out County Road to help his Uncle Jed on his farm.

For years George dreamed of shedding Thornton, Vermont. He

dreamed of adventure and foreign worlds. He pedaled his imagination-fueled starship long after dreams of softer, sweeter adventures crowded the thoughts of the boys he knew from school.

George's father Oscar Cartwright owned Cartwright's Mercantile, which sold everything from hunting rifles to three-piece suits, from household appliances to party dresses, and always had the current Montgomery-Ward catalog available for orders. His mother Eolia, a Boston Adams on her mother's side, dreamed of an elder son who took up the family business and the political mantle of his imagined forebears, but the wide sky called to George in a way that commerce or legislation never could.

Eolia was devastated when George enlisted in the Navy the day after he graduated from Thornton High School, eager to see the world, if not the impossible universe, aboard ship.

He assured her the war was over; and surely the world was ready for peace?

Six years later, his grandfather's copy of *From the Earth to the Moon* lay wrapped in brown paper at the bottom of his Navy-issue duffel, and his elderly seat-mate woke him from dreams of the deadly, churning Sea of Japan off the coast of Korea.

"Thank you, ma'am." George nodded solemnly, gathered his duffel, and made his way off the train.

He scanned the sparse crowd waiting at the station. His brother had been a scrawny fifteen-year-old kid with thick glasses and comic book ink on his fingers, but there was no one waiting who looked he might be a twenty-one-year-old Charlie Cartwright.

George sat himself down in the shade and watched the cars pulling into the station.

The Chevy Bel-Air cruised into the dusty lot like something out of the movies. Two shades of green; one the color of the fir forests he'd missed so badly, the other the color of the sea along Waikiki Beach. The car's sparkling paint was nothing, though, to the pair of legs that swung out of the driver-side door.

Those legs drew his eye over a curving hip and slim waist. Her cap-sleeved dress revealed slender arms and a smooth neck. Her hair was a raven reflection of Marilyn Monroe's, but even Marilyn couldn't hold a candle to this girl's glossy red pout.

She held a hand over her eyes to block the light and looked over the station yard. When her gaze stopped on him, his heart turned over in his chest.

"George?" She called out to him as she walked to him. Her voice was low and warm, a smoky-bar saxophone. "George Cartwright? I'm Ginny Fletcher. Charlie sent me to get you. He had something come up at the store."

George stood, dusting off his khaki trousers and taking the outstretched hand she met him with. She smiled up at him and George's fate was sealed. "The pleasure is all mine, Ginny Fletcher. How is it my brother has such a pretty secretary?"

"Oh, I'm not Charlie's secretary, George." Her laugh, like her voice, was musical. She slipped her arm through his and steered him back towards the waiting Chevy. "I'm his fiancée."

Any words he might have spoken dried up on his tongue.

"Here, sailor." Ginny Fletcher tossed the key to the Bel Air to him. "You remember the way?"

Between the key and the girl, George was out of his depth. Once Ginny was inside the car, he made his way around and into the driver's seat. He eased the Chevy out onto the main road and made his way south towards the bridge.

Ginny opened the lid of a curvy, boxy leather purse on the seat between them and fished around. She caught George's glance. "Change for the toll. A hero shouldn't have to pay his way across the last bridge home."

"So." George cleared his throat. "How long have you and Charlie been engaged?" Ginny Fletcher hadn't been in any of his mother's letters.

Ginny waved her left hand up. On her finger was his grandmother's wedding ring, a Victorian diamond set into a golden buttercup. "Only a week or two. When you telephoned to say you were coming home, your mother was beside herself. Charlie asked me a few days later." Her gaze lingered on the antique stone. "He wanted to have you home to celebrate with us."

"I feel like I missed him growing up," George said wearily. He and his brother had shared an awkward parting hug, and then a handful of letters since George had been gone—all in his first glorious years away, when the world was his front yard, and the idea of going to war again seemed impossible. When there hadn't been a need to come home to see your kid brother graduate, because you might not live to see him again.

With the tollbooth behind them, George swept the car across the expanse of the bridge. "How is he?"

"Swell," Ginny laughed. "Your father keeps him busy at the store, and Charlie hopes—" She broke off and turned to watch Lake Champlain push south toward Mount Independence and Ticonderoga. She turned back to him, resting her hand on the door, fingers dragging in the wind through the open window. "Tell me what he was like as a kid."

"He loved Superman," George began.

Eolia Cartwright was a predictable and unimaginative cook, but George found a kind of comfort in her dry turkey and beige vegetables. The quiet decorum of the dining room he found less comforting. The clink and scrape of forks and stilted attempts at conversation made him homesick for his rack and the boisterous camaraderie of the mess.

Six years had changed nothing in the house on Chapel Street. His mother's tastes were strictly anchored in the rich colors and heavy fabrics of her youth. Here in her sanctuary, the world held fast to a lifestyle a half-century past. George wasn't sure why he'd thought that the coming of the nineteen-fifties would inspire his mother.

She watched him with a zealous intensity, as though he were a project to be managed. His father concentrated on his food with the same single-minded determination he applied to the Mercantile's inventory. Charlie wouldn't meet his eyes.

George scooped up a second helping of buttered turnips and attempted conversation. "So, Mom, you said Aunt Tory had another baby?"

His mother had written to tell him that her sister Victoria, the youngest of Eolia's eleven younger siblings, more than a decade younger than Eolia herself, had given birth to a third child since he'd been away. Three new cousins, this newest one young enough to be his own child.

"His name is Walter, and he has the thickest head of hair I ever saw on a newborn." Eolia smiled fondly. "Now that you're home to stay, you'll be able to get to know them."

His brother reached for his glass. "Are you really home to stay, George?" The question sounded hopeful, but there was something wrong with Charlie's voice. "There's a whole lot of world you haven't seen yet."

"I've seen enough," George said wearily.

Charlie set the glass down on the table with an overloud thump. A slosh of milk rolled over the rim of the glass, spreading damply into the cream damask tablecloth. "When should I plan to be out of the office?" He glared at George over the centerpiece, his blue eyes hard beneath his fashionable Browline frames.

George's hand froze somewhere between his plate and his mouth, the scent of turnips settling uncomfortably in his nose. The pressure of his parents' watchfulness was palpable. He summoned all of his patience to set his fork down gently. "What are you talking about?"

"The Mercantile, George. Your birthright." Spittle gathered in the corner of his little brother's mouth.

Relief pulled at the corner's of George's lips. "I don't want the store, Charlie."

Charlie's puffed-up anger deflated just as Oscar Cartwright's knife toppled off the table, striking the hardwood and bouncing under the credenza. Both men blustered over one another.

"The hell—"

"You don't?"

Eolia reached towards him, but the dining table was too long for her fingers to make contact. "George!"

He set his hands down on either side of his place setting and addressed the hideous oil painting of Ethan Allen and Benedict Arnold that hung over the fireplace. "I don't want the store. I never did. I wanted to travel. And God knows, I've done that."

His father seemed to be mechanically chewing some forgotten mouthful of his dinner. Charlie was still, but his eyes were brittle. His mother's reaching hand retreated to clutch at the pink faux pearls around her neck.

"In fact, I was going to wait until after dinner to tell you all, but I've arranged to start at the college in a few weeks. The Dean feels that after officer training and my six years of service, I should be able to earn my degree in two years, but it will depend on my marks."

"Thornton College?" Eolia's voice rose in surprise. George could almost see the plans swirling in his mother's head when she asked, "What do you plan to study?"

"English literature." He picked up his cutlery and sliced a bite of turkey. Dragging it through the swiftly congealing gravy on his plate, he continued. "I plan to teach after I graduate. Hopefully somewhere nearby, but that will remain to be seen."

"No."

One word in his father's gravelly baritone and the oxygen fled the room. George's head swam.

"No." Oscar Cartwright was flushed, sweat stood out on his gaunt brow. His tone was flat, full of finality. "I did not shepherd the Mercantile through the Depression and the war years to have my son throw it away so he can bury his nose in stories."

"Dad," George said, trying to grasp the truth of his father's outburst, "Hasn't Charlie been running things pretty nicely for you?"

"Your brother," Oscar said without looking at his younger son, "has been a valuable member of the staff, but the Mercantile has been handed from eldest Cartwright son to eldest Cartwright son since my great-grandfather came back from Gettysburg with half a leg and vision for this town's future."

"Doesn't it make more sense to pass it on to the son who wants it?"

"You're the eldest son, George." For his father, the conversation was over.

"Excuse me." Charlie slid his chair back and left the room.

George watched him go. Charlie's gait was stiff, and there was a twitch in his cheek that betrayed his pain. George knew it well from years of fighting off the bigger boys who thought his skinny, awkward younger brother was fair game. Charlie Cartwright wasn't a gangly kid anymore, that much was clear to George. His brother dressed smartly, held an enviable position at the Mercantile, and was engaged to the prettiest girl George had ever seen. Still, he clenched his jaw to push back tears.

Underneath it all, Charlie was still his kid brother.

As a courtesy to their mother, George sat and finished the food on his plate. He'd endured longer meals and faced things more fearful than his father's rage. He cleared his mother's plate in silence, then slipped out the back door into the velvet softness of an August night.

The sunset was peach and azure, the mountains a dusky gray against the darker Eastern sky. From inside the house, the late Hank Williams crooned about a cheating heart.

George hummed along while he walked around the garage, squeezing his now filled-out body between the siding and the hedge. The stack of extra bricks from the patio his father put in when they were kids still lined the back of the garage, and behind the bricks on the bottom left was the Uneeda Biscuit tin George was looking for.

Inside was a six-year-old pack of Lucky Strikes—hidden there by a boy off on a heroic adventure, a boy who never assumed he'd see combat. George envied that boy his innocent secrets.

Overhead, a thick canopy of blaze orange maple leaves filtered the waning sunlight. After six years of palms and scrub firs or endless, treeless skies at sea, their cool embraced him.

The sulfuric snap of the match and the damp burn of the old cigarette filled his nose; the scent was almost enough until the first sweet draw of tobacco flooded his blood. He closed his eyes and fought the sudden urge to get back on the train in Port Henry and ride it wherever it was bound.

"Shh, don't tell." The husky alto pulled him from his thoughts as quickly as soft fingers pulled the smoke from his grip.

George opened his eyes to his cigarette between Ginny Fletcher's perfect lips.

She exhaled slowly and leaned back against the mossy bricks. "Charlie doesn't like the smell, but I'm guessing that's not what drove you out here."

George wished for a coat to lay between her polka-dot dress and the dirty wall. "How did you know I was back here?"

She drew on the cigarette again before handing it back. "I didn't know you were out here. I smelled the cigarette." She dropped her gaze. "I was curious."

George stubbed out the glowing end and stared up at the faint winking of emerging stars. "I've been away a long time."

Ginny's voice drifted alongside his. "Charlie says six years."

"I'm kind of surprised the Luckies survived."

The music in her laugh delighted him. He longed to be one of the funny guys, just to make her laugh all the time.

"I'm picturing you sneaking out here for a smoke with your dad's stolen pin up magazines."

George felt a hot flush up his neck. "I never saw one of those until basic training," he muttered.

"Changed your life, did it?" Ginny giggled.

George couldn't think of a single thing to say. The summer sky offered no assistance.

"I'm sorry." Her jazz voice was gentle now. "I embarrassed you."

"It's nothing."

Ginny reached for his hand. "It's not nothing. I made you uncomfortable. My mother always says, 'Virginia, Charles will think you're fast.'" She pursed her lips in mock disapproval. "I don't think before I talk."

George could feel the pulse dancing under her skin where his thumb grazed her wrist, but he kept his gaze firmly on the heavens. "I don't think that." He waited for her to drop his hand.

She let it rest there in hers. "What do you think?"

The question was almost whispered, and George finally turned to her. She had a smattering of pale freckles on the bridge of her nose and the tips of her dark eyelashes were blond. He could see himself reflected in her green eyes. Hair still Navy short, face more planed and angled than it had been the last time he'd smoked behind the garage, expression more guarded. George resisted threading their fingers together.

"I think Charlie will be looking for his pretty fiancee." George winced inwardly at the forced cheer. He pulled his hand back and pushed up from his slouch against the wall.

Ginny took the hint and dusted her skirt off before leading him back around to the driveway. When George didn't follow her up the front steps, she turned back. "You're not coming in?"

The front door opened and Charlie burst onto the porch. "Ginny, I was wondering where you were. I did promise you a root beer float." He took note of George at the bottom of the steps and his lips turned down petulantly. "I didn't realize you were still here, George."

Ginny laughed. "Your brother is charming, Charlie."

Charlie continued to scrutinize George; whatever he saw there, his expression cleared. He put out an arm for Ginny and ushered her down the stairs and past George. As her slim hand came to rest on Charlie's forearm, Charlie bent to whisper some sweet nothing in her ear.

She smiled tenderly up at his brother, and George felt a pang of pure envy. As they passed him, Charlie gave him a forced grin. "Don't be getting too cozy with my girl."

Ginny glanced at him over her shoulder. George couldn't read her eyes in the half-light.

Two weeks into September, George was questioning the wisdom of his collegiate plan. On the one hand, he kept extremely busy, writing papers to place out of lower level classes and attending his lectures. His mind was full to bursting with words—everyone from Shakespeare to the moderns. Even his beloved Jules Verne had found a place in his studies. On the other hand, his status fell somewhere between Freshman and Junior, and he was about four years and one war too old for carefree mixers and fraternity pledging.

He'd opted to live at home, a situation which was quickly becoming untenable. His mother had decided that he was better suited for the law or medicine, and insisted on discussing those courses of study at every opportunity. Charlie regarded him with suspicion, and his father glowered silently in George's presence.

He'd taken to indulging in a secret cigarette every night after dinner. Though they hadn't seen one another except in passing since the night he arrived home, George couldn't stop thinking about Ginny. At least hiding out behind the garage with his new pack of Lucky Strikes, he could hope she might follow the telltale smoke to his side.

George had pined for home during his years of service, but now that the green canopy above was tinting gold and the winter constellations leaped into the night sky, he realized he no longer belonged anywhere—neither here in the house on Chapel Street nor back on the *Juneau*—neither on the earth nor on the moon.

He was craving that illicit smoke at noon on a bright Wednesday when he passed Ginny Fletcher coming out of Dawson's Grocery. She looked like summer in a red skirt and white blouse, and her nearly black hair was smoothed back in a shiny tail. She was carrying a paper sack of groceries in her arms.

"Ginny!" His greeting startled her; she nearly dropped the bag. George scooped it out of her hands. "What are you shopping for? Bricks?"

She tugged on her ponytail and smoothed her skirt over her hips. "Just a few things for my mother."

"Can I carry them back for you?" George tried to tame the furious roar of blood in his ears. What was it about her that unraveled him?

She tilted her head, and looked up at him from under lowered lashes. "I'd expect nothing less from my future brother-in-law."

Her words gonged in his head. Future brother-in-law. He stepped back to let her lead him. Dawson's was on the same block of College Street as the Ben Franklin, three blocks down from Chapel Street, but George had no idea where Ginny's family lived. "Where are we headed?"

"Just there." Ginny pointed down College Street to the Common. There was only one home on the Common, two of its sides were flanked with shops, the Congregational and Catholic Churches opposed one another, leaving the only remaining space to the imposing three-story, Mansard-style mansion which welcomed all comers to downtown Thornton.

Even as George blurted, "You live there?" he was remembering his mother telling him that Marion Pettengill had passed away a few years back.

"My father bought it two years ago and moved us all here. Basically, he made his fortune and now he intends to let his fortune take care of us." She gave George what he assumed was meant to be a world-weary look. "Investments. Frankly, I think the house is too big and probably haunted."

"Haunted?" George looked at her closely. "Really?"

Her giggle ended in a tiny snort and her ears blushed pink. "No. But it sounds better than 'pretentious and empty.'" She was quiet a moment before asking, "How are your classes?"

"Really great," George said. "They're the only thing I'm certain of right now, except—" *Except that I think I'm falling in love with my brother's girl.*

"Except?" Ginny's eyebrows arched dramatically, and the corners of her smile turned down teasingly.

"Except that..." He cast into his mind for a distraction and came up with the only other constant in his life. "I still love Jules Verne more than any other writer. Maybe even more than Shakespeare." For the second time in as many conversations, George felt his face and neck burning with shame.

"Let me guess," Ginny began, pausing at the corner of College and Chapel. George took her arm with his free one and escorted her across the street. "*20,000 Leagues* is your favorite."

"No." George grinned. No one ever guessed.

"*Five Weeks in a Balloon?*"

"No." Another corner of George's traitorous heart declared for Ginny. She knew Jules Verne.

Ginny's playful expression went serious as they walked over the grassy Common toward her family's home. George's pulse hammered. She took his measure deliberately while the sunlight dappled her hair. The green-tinted sunlight was too bright, the fresh-cut grass too sharp in his nose. The town common was suddenly as vast and foreign as the Pacific or the surface of the faraway moon.

"I've got it!" Ginny tugged on his arm. Her triumphant grin lit up the afternoon. "*Around the World in 80 Days!*"

George laughed out loud. Her nose wrinkled when he shook his head; if it was possible for a girl like Ginny Fletcher to look like a schoolmarm, she did.

Ginny narrowed her eyes. "Are you pulling my leg?"

"No." He hoisted the sack of groceries up a little.

"What is it?"

His next words slipped out before he could catch them. "You're pretty when you're flustered."

Her eyes widened at the compliment. For a heartbeat, her fluttering lashes and teasing mouth were still. She composed herself and flashed him a steely glance, softened by playful humor in her emerald eyes. "I'll figure it out, you know."

"I don't doubt it."

They had reached the front porch of the Pettengill House—the Fletcher House now, he supposed.

Ginny reached out for the groceries. "Thank you for walking me home, George."

He brushed her bare arms handing over the paper bag and shivered at the feel of her sun-warm skin. Her lips parted over a quick indrawn breath and George was undone.

"My pleasure, Ginny." He leaned in and kissed her cheek. If his lips lingered too long, too close to the tempting corner of her lips, neither of them gave breath to the thought.

Ginny left him with a Mona Lisa smile, the front door closing softly between them.

He was halfway back across the Common before his feet touched the ground.

A cocktail of guilt and desire fizzed in George's blood through the darkening days of autumn. The foliage burned from amber to crimson, leaving an ashy grayness over November. In the hopes of securing a room of his own somewhere for the second semester, he took a job as a farmhand at his aunt and uncle's dairy. It was cold, exhausting, early morning work, and in combination with the endless reading and writing for his degree, George found he could keep improper thoughts of Ginny Fletcher at bay, though he saw her regularly enough.

She came to Sunday dinner every week, and every week Eolia seated her to George's left, safely across the table from Charlie, in an effort to maintain an antique decorum. George barely tasted these meals; the entire force of his being was concentrated on not betraying his deepening feelings for his brother's fiancée.

He would take note of Charlie and Ginny's presence around town with a stunted smile and some inane pleasantry.

George was the only one in the family actually relieved that Ginny's parents had accepted Oscar and Eolia's invitation to join them for Thanksgiving dinner. Knowing he wouldn't be the only one eating under unbearable strain gave him a grim satisfaction.

The conversation around the holiday table happened in hands like a card game. Oscar and Alfred Fletcher would discuss business, stocks, weather, and war for a few moments. Eolia would attempt to engage Bea Fletcher in some gossip to diffuse the heated male topics. Bea, who didn't tend to mingle much, would nod while Eolia floundered. Ginny would praise Charlie's innovations at the Mercantile or ask George about his courses at Thornton to relieve her mother, and the older men would steamroll over the young men's answers, bringing the whole farce round again.

George wanted a cigarette. Badly.

Eolia was about to get up for the coffee service when Charlie stood. The scraping of his chair on the hardwood startled Oscar and Alfred Fletcher into silence.

Eolia sat again. "Charlie?"

Charlie looked at Ginny across the table. Her expression was guarded.

"Ginny and I have set a date for the wedding."

Eolia beamed. "When, dears?"

The Fletchers watched Charlie very carefully. George wanted to sink through the floor.

"June 11, 1955."

Eolia's face crumpled. Seeing Charlie and Ginny's dismay and the bland acceptance on the Fletchers' faces, she pasted her smile back on quickly. "Why such a long engagement, Charlie?"

Ginny jumped in to save Charlie. "We're going to wait until Mr. Cartwright retires and Charlie has enough put by for a house of our own."

"Did I say I was retiring in 1955, Charles?" Oscar's voice was deadly quiet, and though he addressed Charlie, it was George he looked at.

"Sure, Dad," Charlie blustered. "You told Ed Pease you were going to retire in two years. At the Memorial Day barbecue."

Oscar held the table still with his silence. His eyes never left George, who stared back, waiting for his father to speak.

"I did tell Ed Pease I was going to retire in two years." He paused to let the statement sink in. "When George had had enough time to take over the business."

"Jesus Christ, Dad!" Charlie exploded. "George doesn't even want the business!" His chair clattered to the floor in his rush to escape the dining room.

Ginny set her napkin on the table. "Excuse me, Mrs. Cartwright." She ran out in Charlie's wake.

George said nothing, holding his father's gaze.

Bea Fletcher cleared her throat. Her flutey voice piped up uncertainly. "Fred, dear, I think we should excuse ourselves. Eolia, dinner was lovely. Thank you so much for having us."

Alfred pulled her chair out for her and they, too, vanished into the hall.

"George," Oscar began, but Eolia interrupted.

"Surely this can wait, Oscar?"

George's father snapped at his wife, but George intervened. "No, Mother. It needs to be said now." He stood, speaking formally to his father.

"Dad, I am going to finish my degree and take a teaching position. I have no plans to join the business. Charlie loves the Mercantile, and by all evidence, he's going to do well by it. You need to stop this. I'm going to excuse myself." He leaned over the corner of the table to kiss his mother's cheek. "Mother, thank you for dinner."

George didn't expect to find Ginny behind the garage with his Lucky Strikes, but that didn't dampen his disappointment when she wasn't there.

He leaned and smoked in the damp afternoon chill. The day was drizzly and overcast, the high somewhere in the forties. He hadn't thought to stop for his coat, so the relatively mild weather was a blessing. When his father's car started up two slow cigarettes later, George assumed Oscar was headed to the American Legion Post for Scotch and soda and commiseration.

Thinking the coast was clear, George slipped in the kitchen door, thinking to help his mother in the kitchen. Instead, he found Charlie, alone with a bottle. The condensation from his highball glass pooled on the faded linoleum tabletop. The leftovers congealed quietly on the counters, hip to shoulder with stacks of the family's good china and silver.

"You should just take it," Charlie whimpered into his whiskey on the rocks. "He'll die before he lets me have it. No matter that we've made more money since I started working there than we did for years before that."

"I don't want it, Charlie." George took a second highball glass from the cabinet and poured himself a splash of his brother's Canadian blend, neat. "I want you to have it. I told Dad after you walked out, I'm not coming into the business."

Charlie was well nigh onto drunk. "Doesn't matter that I talked Fred Fletcher into backing the expansion into television sets or that Fred's connections have secured some better prices from some of our major suppliers." He downed his drink and poured another in rapid succession. "Doesn't mean a damn thing that I come in early and stay late every day." He looked up with bleary eyes. "Doesn't matter that when Fred and Bea Fletcher die I'll be the heir to all their money. I'm marrying the Mercantile's insurance policy and our old man doesn't give a shit."

George's head spun from revelation and liquor; nicotine and dry turkey twisted in his gut and he worried he might toss the whole mess up. He took the bottle from Charlie's hand. "You're pretty drunk, Charlie."

"Not too drunk to see how you look at her, brother."

George stood, taking the whiskey bottle with him. "Go to bed, Charlie."

Charlie stumbled up, leaning hard on the door jamb. "I see how you look at her."

Christmas was a broken affair.

It snowed on Christmas Eve, blanketing Thornton overnight in four inches of sparkling white. The Cartwrights attended services in the morning and dutifully gathered around the tinseled tree afterwards to celebrate.

Eolia bought and wrapped gifts from each of her sons to their father, and from Oscar to his sons. As was their custom, Oscar and Eolia exchanged token gifts from the Mercantile's inventory. For Eolia, a bottle of Yardley English Lavender, for Oscar a new pair of black leather gloves.

George had brought back gifts from his last stopover in Honolulu, but the gesture fell flat amongst his family's silent war. His mother let him clasp a bracelet of Hawaiian pearls around her wrist with a wistful sigh. He'd brought Charlie home a tiki idol, guaranteed by the weathered carver to bring luck to the recipient. Charlie said *thank you*, but George heard the doubt in his brother's voice.

His father grunted in his general direction at the carefully selected koa-wood box George had envisioned on his father's desk in the Mercantile's office.

They ate gray roast beef and soggy Yorkshire pudding in miserable silence, after which George excused himself from yet another holiday table.

He fled on foot down Chapel Street, turning right without a glance across the street at Cartwright's Mercantile, standing dark on the opposite corner. He stopped on the stone bridge which spanned the spot where the Thorn River bisected downtown and dropped over the falls, spilling and foaming on its way north towards Lake Champlain. College Street was quiet save for the small crowd entering the Congregational Church on that side of the Common.

George stood for a long time, watching the water tumble past the ice that formed on the stone legs of the bridge, feeling the spray sting his cheeks. When he looked up, it was snowing again.

"Merry Christmas, George!" Ginny was running down the side-walk, feet sure in sturdy snow boots.

Warmth bloomed in his chest; there was nothing he could do to stop it. Ginny wore a bright blue wool coat and a yellow knit tam and scarf. Her dark hair and scarlet lips brought out the green in her eyes and the flush on her cheeks. She shone like a string of Christmas lights, haloed by swirling flurries. In her gloved hands was a small package wrapped in festive printed paper.

One look at the despair in George's eyes and she reached up to touch his face. "What is it?"

He leaned into her palm, savoring her heat through the wool gloves. "It's everything, Ginny. And it's nothing."

"It's not Charlie's fault," she said gently.

"I know," he replied. "I think."

Ginny pressed the package into his hands. "I saw you while I was out with the carolers. I ran home to get this for you. I'll give Charlie his gift when he comes for dinner—"

George was delighted and terribly embarrassed. "You got me a Christmas gift?"

"I figured you out. I told you I would." The smile she gave him was playful and knowing. "Open it."

"Here?"

"Yes."

George untied the ribbon and stuffed it in his coat pocket, then tore through the wrapping. Inside was the vanilla-and-history smell of old books. *Around the Moon*, by Jules Verne. Ginny opened the cover. Lying against the frontispiece was a note on her stationery.

Dearest George,

Your favorite is From the Earth to the Moon. *I should have known all along. You are a dreamer, a traveler, a man of words.*

I always wanted to know what happened to the moon adventurers, but I'd never read the sequel.

I know you don't have this edition in your collection. I asked your mother.

Merry Christmas, Ginny

He looked at the publishing page. A first edition of the English translation. "Ginny, it's wonderful. Thank you."

She wrapped her hands around his, holding the book between them. She had to tip her head to look up at him. "You're very welcome."

A recklessness grew in his chest. "Do you love him?"

Ginny blinked. Something dark flashed in her eyes and she hesitated. Snowflakes landed on her cheeks and eyelashes. "Your brother's a good man. I made him promises, George."

He held tight to her hands, wishing there weren't two thick layers between them. "I love you, Ginny. I love you."

Tears welled in her eyes, washing the snow away as they fell. "Oh, George."

Before he could second-guess himself, he tugged her gently closer, both of them still clutching the book. When his lips touched hers, he swore he heard music. Her mouth stiffened in shock, then softened briefly against his.

Every kiss George had known before went up in flames. For those heartbeats, the world spun around Ginny Fletcher, and he knew he'd never love another girl the same way.

He felt her pull back. George kept his eyes closed; he simply couldn't bear to see her walk away.

When he opened his eyes, Ginny was gone, absorbed into the group of carolers spilling out of the church.

George returned to classes in January determined to banish Ginny from his heart. To that end, he went to the mixers with friends from his classes. He shed his fear of being the old guy and asked a girl to the movies. On his best days, it almost worked.

At the end of the month, he came home to find Ginny's bright blue coat on the hall tree. The memory of their kiss in the snow scattered his carefully constructed resolve and he strained to hear her voice.

From the sounds of it, she was having late-afternoon coffee and cookies with his mother. George could hear Eolia prattle on about Ginny's trousseau while he divested himself of his winter clothes in the front hall.

Ginny blushed over her cup when George answered his mother's summons to the parlor.

"There's a letter for you in the kitchen, dear."

The letter was from Bert Napoli, a sailor he'd come up through basic with. There was a Boston postmark.

Dear George,

I hope this finds you well. I should have written sooner, but I've been on the road since I dropped you at the train station. I made my way to Boston these last six months doing some odd jobs for my uncle. I am staying with some cousins with business concerns here in Massachusetts and thinking I may stay on. If you ever come to Boston, they know how to have a good time.

Which brings me to why I'm writing. It's a small world, George. Last week I was with my cousin Gianni at a party and I met a guy named Charlie Cartwright from Vermont. I overheard him telling Gianni about his brother George coming home from the Navy, and I knew he had to mean you. Your sister-in-law is a firecracker. If Loretta has any sisters, I'm coming up there instead. Who knew they grew girls like that in cow land?

I hope you've got one like her to keep you warm. These New England winters are no joke.

Best, Bert

His sister-in-law? Loretta?

George's first reaction was that Bert must have met another Charlie Cartwright with a brother George in the Navy, but the uglier truth kept asserting itself.

Charlie had been in Boston on store business the previous week; he'd even mentioned going to a party. He hadn't mentioned Bert Napoli, but Bert had always been able to fade out of sight when he wanted to. George folded the letter carefully and slipped it into his shirt pocket, then went back out to the front hall for his coat and boots.

He found Charlie in the smaller office off the store room in the basement. Their father's office was on the main floor of the Mercantile, with his door open to the store and in full view of the front counter.

George didn't knock. "Who's Loretta?"

Charlie dropped his pen, but gathered it up deliberately before meeting George's glare. "She's nobody. A good-time girl I see some-times when I'm in Boston. She spends my money on cocktails and cigarettes and she does things in bed girls like Ginny won't ever even know exist."

George felt sucker-punched. "Does she know you're engaged?"

Charlie laughed, but it was a bitter, hollow sound. "She knows. Doesn't give a damn. I'm not her steady guy or anything. She's prob-ably got a dozen guys like me on a line." He shuffled a stack of papers. "Loretta's got nothing to do with me and Ginny. Got it?"

"Jesus, Charlie. Ginny thinks the world of you."

"Let's just keep it that way, okay?" Charlie got up from behind the cramped desk, nearly banging his head on the hanging lamp. He closed in on George. "Ginny and the Fletchers are the best thing I've got, my only shot at making something of myself." He punched George harder than playfully in the arm. "Since the old man doesn't exactly support me around here."

"What happened to you, Charlie?"

Charlie pushed his glasses up on his nose, a nervous gesture George knew well from their childhood. "My big brother ran off to be a hero, and I had to grow up fast." He brushed past George, pausing at the office door. "Don't mess with me and Ginny, George. I'm not letting her go."

Just over two weeks later, George waited in the lobby of the women's residence for Jeannie Snow. He'd had a haircut and picked up a rose corsage. After Bert's letter and his conversation with Charlie, he'd doubled his resolve to forget his brother's fiancée, complete the semester at Thornton College, and transfer to another school to finish his degree. He needed to get out of his hometown before he spoiled everything.

Taking Jeannie to the American Legion Valentine's Day Dance was mostly for show, to prove to his brother he didn't want to rock the boat. She was a nice girl, a sophomore from New Jersey majoring in

French. George tried to ignore that if you caught her out of the corner of your eye, her dark hair and slim form bore some resemblance to Ginny Fletcher.

Jeannie accepted her flower with coquettish eyelashes and filled the walk through downtown to the Legion Hall with easy chatter about their classmates and her French classes. He knew there were guys who were jealous of Jeannie's interest in him, guys who would gladly fill his shoes once he eventually told her she was sweet, but that he wasn't looking for a steady thing.

The hall was festooned in pink and red hearts and flowers. George had a grim chuckle at his father's expense. Oscar would loathe the use of the Legion Hall for a dance like this, but the sales from tickets and cups of frothy pink punch, thick with halved strawberries, orange slices, and lemon sherbet, funded the post's costs.

Jeannie kept him on his toes, literally. The four-piece band only played old standards, but Jeannie didn't care. She loved to dance, and had the ability to make him feel like a less awkward leader than he was.

George barely managed to keep from watching his brother's fiancée laugh and twirl in Charlie's arms. Charlie's table was full of a changing crowd of admirers. George suspected he was spiking their punch. Ginny wore red that matched her lipstick, with poppies in her hair that Charlie had bought for her at the florist.

For one brief moment, she'd felt the weight of his regard. She caught his gaze from underneath lowered lashes, and her eyes flicked towards the dance floor. George sighed and shook his head imperceptibly.

When Jeannie felt his attention wane, she dragged him back onto the dance floor, coaxing out his smile with her easy humor. As the dance wound down, George was almost surprised to realize he'd enjoyed himself.

He walked Jeannie back to her dormitory, down College Street and over the Thorn River. He kissed Jeannie's cheek at the door and waited until she blinked the desk lamp in her window before he turned back for town. Her cheek had been cold against his still glove-warm palm, but when he reached back into his pocket for his gloves, they were tangled in a length of red ribbon, and Ginny was right there in his thoughts again.

When he saw the blue coat on the bridge, he cursed himself for a fool. There was no way to avoid her without crossing the street in full view and walking around her. George dropped his chin into the folds of his scarf and pushed his hands down deep into his coat pockets.

"Ginny," he said politely, passing her with a nod.

"George?" The questioning tilt of her head dropped a curled lock of hair against her cheek. "You're not going to talk to me?"

He stopped a few feet past her and turned back. "It's late."

"And you don't have a curfew." Her brow knotted. "Keep me company a bit, George. It's the least you can do after ignoring me all evening at the Legion Hall."

He took a single step in her direction. "You and Charlie were having a fine time."

Ginny shifted so they were closer. "So were you, with that coed."

The sky was clear overhead, the river below bubbling under skims and floes of ice, save where its static whisper whooshed over the falls. George gave up and pulled her into his arms.

"Ginny, you know how I feel about you. Don't toy with me. Tell Charlie you love me, too, and we'll get out of here. We'll get married and go somewhere new."

For one mad heartbeat he saw yes in her eyes. He saw the whole future spin out, fleeing town on a Greyhound bus and starting out fresh. Sadness shuttered Ginny's expression again, and George knew it had passed. He released her, but she didn't step back.

"I made promises, George. I believe in those promises." She didn't reach for him this time. There was too much at stake. "Someday you'll think of me as a sister, and we'll laugh about this madness."

"Damn it, Ginny," he growled, dragging her up against him and locking his arms around her. "I'll never think of you like a sister."

His mouth closed over hers and he tasted lemon sherbet from the Legion Hall. She made a small sound in the back of her throat and clung to him, lips curving and yielding. She wound her gloved fingers into his hair and kissed him back. He poured his longing into that kiss, cherishing her even as he took his pleasure.

They came apart breathing hard. Ginny backed away from him, wide-eyed and flushed, and the reality of how far over the line he'd gone crashed down on him.

He turned on his heel and rushed through the slush for the house on Chapel Street.

In the spring, his Aunt Tory and Uncle Jed offered him their spare bedroom and two meals a day instead of cash in exchange for his work at the farm. George missed the pocket money, but the relief of leaving the house on Chapel Street was palpable. He picked up a shift at the college library to pay for his lunches and the occasional date. He bought a used bicycle and rode it daily, save when the snow was bad.

The drudgery seemed a fitting penance for his sins, and his new home outside of town meant fewer opportunities to run into Ginny.

His grades, always strong, improved even further, launching him to the top of his classes.

Spring bloomed, and with it came the news that the Dean approved George's plan to finish his degree a semester early. George was over the moon. Jeannie Snow, whom he'd been dating when his schedule allowed, insisted they go see a movie and get a celebratory milkshake.

When he dropped her off at the residence hall, he was feeling oddly melancholy. Jeannie was happy for him and proud of his hard work. She'd told everyone at the diner about his advancement, even getting the patrons to raise a toast, but the victory felt hollow. His earlier resolve to leave town would be wasted, given that he could get the degree faster if he stayed put, but what to do afterwards?

George suspected that Jeannie was starting to have opinions about his future. That feeling lodged like a stone in his chest.

The woman he most wanted to share his news with was the last woman in the world he should go anywhere near, but his traitorous feet took him straight to her door the very next afternoon. He hadn't meant to, but he'd come into town in the Fuller's pickup truck to fetch some aspirin for little Walter's chest cold, and the Pettengill—Fletcher—House had called to him from its place on the Common.

He rang the bell with his heart in his throat and his hat in his hands. Bea Fletcher answered the door.

"Oh, hello George," she said.

He clasped the Fedora behind his back to hold himself still. "Good afternoon, Mrs. Fletcher. Is Ginny home?"

Bea's face fell. "Oh, no, dear. Ginny's gone up to Burlington with her father to see about a proper church for the wedding. Fred and I just think we won't be able to fit everyone in the church here. And there's nowhere for a reception..." Mrs. Fletcher's train of thought petered out. "Shall I tell her you called?"

"No, ma'am. I'll catch up with her another time." He replaced the hat, tipped the brim, and trotted down the porch steps. Walking across the Common in May sunshine, George decided to pay his mother a visit. She would at least pretend to be proud of him.

He was surprised to hear shouting when he turned the corner onto Chapel Street. He was even more surprised when the shouting was coming through the open windows of his parents' front parlor.

His father was home, and roaring like a wounded bear. "You'll marry her, Charles, or you'll never set foot in my store again."

George slipped up the front steps and through the front door, pausing in the doorway when he heard the wet sniffle of a crying female.

"Young lady," his mother's voice now, but cold and purposeful, "are you absolutely certain?"

A ringing honk into a hankie, and a coarse, broad-voweled reply, "I'm not that kind of girl, Mrs. Cartwright. Charlie told me he loved me."

"Dad, she's lying. She's known the whole time I was going to marry Ginny."

The crying woman started sobbing. Oscar Cartwright bellowed and George heard something glass shatter inside the parlor. "How does that make it acceptable, what you've done?" When there was no reply from his younger son Oscar spoke more measuredly. George was frozen in place, waiting to see what would happen.

"You'll marry Loretta in the morning, Charles. I'll see to it with Reverend Beacham, and you'll move into one of the apartments over the store. You'll continue to manage the daily running of the store, but there won't be any more trips. I'll handle that myself. You can't be trusted."

"Dad—" Charlie's voice sounded strangled.

"Furthermore, you'll march yourself over to the Fletchers' house this very evening and explain what you've done. If you're lucky," his father dropped his voice to a horrible menacing growl, "Fred Fletcher will shoot you and this whole mess will be over for all of us."

George's stomach clenched when Loretta wailed in misery. Their father had Charlie pinned. He wouldn't walk away from the store; he'd marry his good-time girl and her baby would be a Cartwright. George knew that in his bones.

Oh, Ginny. His heart hoped and ached for her.

He backed out of the door, twisting the knob so the door would snug into the frame silently. The last thing his little brother needed was the further humiliation of knowing George had heard the whole thing. When the locked snicked imperceptibly shut, George released a breath he hadn't been aware of holding.

He turned to face Ginny, who stood on the porch, fingers clenched around the back of a wooden rocking chair. Her lips were white, her skin bleached, eyes sparkling with pain.

"Ginny."

She bolted, skirts swishing around her calves. George started after her, but Charlie's voice stopped him cold.

"Don't you dare."

George spun around. "You're in no position to stop me."

A blond in a pencil skirt and tottering heels with a voice like bubble gum clattered out behind Charlie. "Chas?"

George stepped down onto the walkway. The rest of his life

opened up beyond the front gate of the house on Chapel Street. He just needed to find Ginny.

"I love her, Charlie. I love her, and I'm going after her."

George caught up with Ginny on the bridge. He grabbed her hand and she stumbled around and into his arms. Her eyes were red-rimmed from crying, her makeup smeared. The bright, overcast sky intensified the colors around them, and the falls underneath roared in his ears.

Passersby dodged them. He heard the beginnings of whispers as they passed.

He couldn't have said what he expected to find in her face, but anger wasn't it.

"Did you know?" Her voice broke over the words, but she held herself together.

George thought of the letter from Bert, folded into his copy of Around the Moon, stacked on the tiny desk in his room at the Fullers'. Ginny heard the truth in his silence.

"You knew. You knew he had some girl on the side." She shoved him away, grief twisting her features. "You told me you loved me, George."

"I do." His hands fell to his side. "God knows I do."

"How could you let him do this to me?" She was pleading with him. "To us?"

"Us?" Under the shame and the guilt, a spark kindled.

Ginny edged away, gripping the wall. "How long?"

"I don't know. Long enough," George muttered.

"No." She spoke without looking at him. "How long have you known?"

The spark guttered. "Since January."

Truth and betrayal spiraled out over the river. The future he'd felt blossoming was tumbling into the thrashing waters of the Thorn River. He was losing her.

"Ginny." He laid his hand over hers, clasping her fingers. George held her hand in silence until he felt a slight give in her bones. Gently he turned her to face him. "Virginia Fletcher, I love you. I have since the moment you stepped out of your father's Bel Air in Port Henry, and I'll never love another girl this way as long as I live."

He dropped to his knees on the sidewalk. There were tears streaming over her cheeks, pooling in the soft corners of her lips and tracing the curve of her chin and jaw.

"I wanted to tell you everything, but you'd made it so clear, that you were going to be with my brother. I didn't think it was my place, especially when everything I knew was hearsay." He paused for a breath. Her tears hadn't slowed, but like the sun behind a rain cloud, there was light in her eyes. "I'll explain everything, but Ginny, I have to know."

His heart slammed in his chest. Hope waited like a mine in his chest.

"Do you love me?"

She wrapped his arms around her waist, and he laid his cheek against the pleats of her skirt. "I do love you, George."

He leaned back to see her face, streaked with weeping and mascara, and never more beautiful. He stood, slowly becoming aware of the crowd building around them as his hope exploded into joy.

"I love you, George." She threw herself into his arms, whispering through her tears. "From the earth to the moon."

~

From the World of Thornton Vermont

CINNAMON GIRL

CAMERON D. GARRIEPY

When Walt Fuller's father dropped dead repairing a pasture fence a week before Thanksgiving, his mother went into a period of mourning that lasted until the day she died. Jed's broad-chested, bull-headed life had been the center of hers, and when his light went out, Tory Fuller switched hers off as well.

Walt missed his Pop something fierce, but his grief was overshadowed by the sheer size of his mother's pain.

Within a day, the three bedroom farmhouse on the Fuller's dairy farm was full to brimming with funereal closeness. His oldest sister Patty came up from Connecticut with her husband and the babies and set up camp in the spare room. Uncles, aunts, cousins, and friends poured in; the house swelled up with grief and goodwill. His brother was sleeping in his camper in the driveway, but he still came in to eat and use the toilet.

Walt couldn't say for sure if Joe was showering at all.

He lasted three days among the mourners before taking his Pop's truck west on County Road and driving until he could breathe again. A few yards shy of the Lake Champlain bridge, the truck ran out of gas. Cursing both the rare impulse and his father's unexpected death, Walt hopped out of the truck to hitch a ride home.

If his fingers hadn't been nearly frozen in the pockets of his Levis, the snow-scented wind off Lake Champlain would have made him smile. Walt relished the anticipation of long, dark Vermont winters. The dormant silence of a frozen pasture at dawn eased him in a way even the calving and greening of spring never could. The bovine warmth of the twilight barns comforted him like the drafty farmhouse never had.

He was contemplating the far-distant top of the Crown Point light house memorial when a blue Beetle honked and pulled onto the gravel shoulder. The girl who pushed out of the car had hair the color of cinnamon that curled out of her wool cap, and curves her bell-bottoms and a fair-isle ski sweater did nothing to hide. She came around the backside of the bug and leaned a hip against the rear hatch.

"Need a ride?" Her clear blue eyes were sparkling with suppressed laughter, taking in his truck and lack of a jacket.

The driver waved her hand. She was singing along with ABBA's "Dancing Queen," drumming delicately on the steering wheel of the VW.

Cinnamon Girl grinned, returned to the open passenger side door, and pushed her seat forward to open up the back. "By the way, that's Jane, and I'm Molly."

Walt arranged his limbs in the back of Jane's bug. The car was cramped, and his knees pressed into the seats. He rested one arm on one of about a half dozen paper bags crammed in with him.

"Where to?" Molly shifted in her seat to crane her neck. Her eyes crinkled when she smiled.

"Fuller Farm. It"s just—"

"Up County Road another coupl'a miles," Jane said. She half-turned to Molly as she eased the VW back onto the road. "You must be Walt."

He blinked at the girl driving. She was blonde-haired, blue-eyed, pretty in a catalog kind of way. "Ayuh."

He heard his father in the old-timer response, and his chest squeezed.

Molly giggled, still twisted around to watch him. "Jane's mom works at Town Hall. She knows everyone."

Jane's gaze flicked to Walt in the rearview mirror. "I'm sorry about your father."

A cloud of concern passed across Molly's face. "Oh, I—"

He cut off Molly's sympathy. "Thanks."

Molly reached out an arm, laying her slightly freckled hand on his knee. He felt the warmth of that touch through his flannel-lined denim. "Really. I'm sorry, too."

Her crinkly eyes were wide with sympathy. It was too much. "So, where were you heading? Before you rescued me?"

"Jane came to get me for Thanksgiving break," Molly said. "I'm doing my last semester at Empire State in Saratoga Springs."

"We're cousins." Jane's eyes stayed on the road.

The bags in the backseat made a little more sense. "Do you always pack in grocery sacks?"

Molly's answering laugh was deep and true; Walt wanted to make her laugh again.

Jane sighed. "She's hopeless."

Molly wrapped her arms around the headrest and laid her cheek on the seat with a helpless grin. "My laundry bag ripped."

Jane slowed the car, turning into the driveway at the farm. He caught her slightly narrowed glance at his brother's derelict camper, huddled amongst a jumble of cars, and felt an answering stain rise up the back of his neck. As soon as the car stopped, he leaned forward in anticipation of escaping.

Molly opened her door and climbed out, flipping the lever to release the passenger seat as she did. Walt pushed it forward and crawled out of the little blue car. He turned, ducking down to address Jane. "Thanks for the ride."

Jane gave him a pitying half-smile. When he straightened, Molly's gaze was waiting. "I'll be home all week. Maybe I'll see you around."

He pushed his bare hands deep into his pockets. He meant to say, "Going to be busy with all this family, the funeral..." What came out sounded a lot like, "Maybe."

Jed Fuller was laid to rest the Sunday after Thanksgiving.

Nearly everyone in Thornton was there at the burial ground on Fuller Creek Road. To Molly it seemed half of Vermont was huddled there by the half-frozen creek, heads bowed around the Fuller family stone while Reverend Shutter prayed for Jed's immortal soul, though his body would wait in the crypt until spring.

Jane shivered next to her, immaculately turned out in a black dress and what Molly thought of as her Sunday coat, though she'd decided on her snow boots. For her own part, Molly had squeezed into something borrowed from her mother, and covered it up with her parka after the service in town.

Walt stood between his mother and a slightly older young woman Molly assumed was his sister. Jane had given her a primer on the family before they'd come, even while she'd tried to talk Molly out of it. "We don't even know him," she'd said.

"He needs friends," was all Molly could think to reply. Watching him shoulder a corner of his father's casket, a clutch of idle snowflakes sticking to his lashes, Molly stood by her assessment.

The half-hearted snow swirled into a squall just as Reverend Shutter concluded his prayers, and Walt looked up. She smiled at him through the rioting snow, but wasn't sure he saw.

At the farm, Jane found Bobby's parents, who drew her into their circle of friends. Molly drifted past the dining room table, stopping to take a cider donut and a cup of coffee. She paused to say hello to some neighbors, but it was Walt she sought out while they spoke.

She found him sitting on the stairs, his coat still folded in his lap. "Hi," she said. "How are you holding up?"

"All right, I guess." He blinked at her, and Molly was painfully aware of the fact that they'd only just met. "How did you know about the funeral?"

"Jane." Molly broke the donut in half and offered him a piece. "She drove, too. I hope it's okay."

Walt took the donut; their fingers brushed, and her insides went warm. For a moment, though, he only held it, staring at a point on the wall just beyond her.

She finished the donut to fill the awkward silence, but then there was cinnamon sugar on her fingertips, and she'd forgotten to bring a napkin. In desperation, she licked her fingertips, then grinned at her own foolishness. She didn't have a napkin. "I'm sorry. I'm intruding."

"You're not—" he began. A tentative smile played around his mouth—probably at her expense, but she'd take it—then his sister's voice rang out, challenging his assertion.

"Walter? Where are you? Sal and Rachel are getting ready to leave."

Walt's eyes followed the sound of his sister's voice to the front hall, where an elderly couple were bundling up. He shook his head just a tiny bit, blushing a little when she caught it and gave him an answering wry smile.

"I am," she said stepping back to let him by. As he passed she brushed his hand with hers. "See you around."

Jane was easy to find; she was even easier to convince to leave.

Molly shed her jacket and tossed it in the back of Jane's car. "He's like a lost puppy."

Jane sighed as Molly's coat tumbled off the seat, then turned the car around and pulled away. "He's a dairy farmer, Moll. Don't you want something nicer?"

"Don't be a snob." Molly reached for the radio dial. "You're only doing secretarial training so you can work for Bobby's dad and save up for a house faster."

Jane's disapproving frown flipped, and she flexed her left hand. The light caught the small diamond solitaire Bobby Thompson had put on her finger three months before. She looked up at Molly sharply. "So, why did you bother to do four years of college?"

"It's 1977, Janey. I want to learn things, just to learn them. I want to figure out where I belong. You know?" Molly glanced in the rearview mirror at the receding farm. "In case you didn't notice, I've hardly been a man-magnet in Saratoga Springs."

"At least Walt Fuller has the good sense to think you're pretty," Jane conceded.

A happy shiver coursed down Molly's spine. "Do you think so?"

"Don't be stupid. I saw how he looked at you that day on the bridge."

Molly sighed. With her long, thick blonde hair and blue eyes, Jane Starr was the kind of girl guys just noticed. Molly's not-quite-red unruly waves that curled near her face, her curves, and her earnest face were more sidekick than leading lady.

The way he'd looked at her that day by the bridge had made her feel like the leading lady. She'd liked his eyes—serious and gray-hazel--and the appreciation in them.

"You know, Moll," Jane said, pulling the car into Molly's driveway. "Walt Fuller has something going for him."

"Yeah?" Molly reached for her coat.

Jane shrugged. "He's probably got a house already."

"Patty, why are we doing this again?" Walt trudged through the rows of blue spruce with his sister while his niece and nephew covered one another in snow and fallen needles.

Patty grinned. "Because Mom's not home to remind you, I'm leaving in three days, and we'll be with Gary's family for Christmas, and Joe will probably forget what day it is. If we don't get you a Christmas tree now, you won't have one at all, and that's just sad." She stopped, hands on her hips, and peered through the row at an eight footer a few feet away. "That one."

Walt followed the line of her gaze and approached the tree in question. "This one?"

"Yes." One of the kids squealed from somewhere behind them, and Patty hollered back without looking. "Leave your sister alone."

Walt knelt under the tree, shaking some of the snow off the boughs before he notched the hand saw into the bark. "You know mom's going to stay with Aunt Yolie. There's no point in a tree at the farm."

His sister was uncharacteristically silent. He heard her boots crunching through the snow toward him. Her voice, when she spoke, was gentle. "Mom can't hide herself away with at Yolie's for the rest of her life."

Walt finished notching the tree, then eased out from underneath it to hand the saw to Patty. "Hold that."

Patty took the saw. "Okay, fine. Mom probably will stay with Yolie in town."

Walt took the saw back and crawled under on the other side of the trunk to finish the job.

"You could always invite that pretty redhead from the funeral over to help you trim your tree."

Walt's head snapped up and he thwacked it on a low branch, muttering a curse in Patty's direction as the remaining snow in the boughs fell on him with a soft *whump*.

Patty and the kids laughed; Walt couldn't help grinning at himself. "Thanks, Sissy. I needed that."

"The laugh or the tree?" Patty asked, nudging her kids back into the snow to play.

Walt looked between the kids wrestling in the dirty track and his sister standing over the fallen fir, and channeled the memory of his Pop—intentionally this time. "Ayuh."

Patty's eyes misted over. "Let's get this tree back to the truck." She brushed away the emotion and hollered again at the kids. "Ellen, Alex, back to the truck!"

Walt grabbed the tree by a lower branch and dragged it along. When he caught up to Patty, she gave him a sly look.

"Who is the redhead anyhow?"

His cold-stung cheeks warmed a bit. "Molly Sanders."

"She's pretty. How'd you meet?"

"You remember the day I stranded the truck out by the bridge?" He paused; Patty nodded. "Molly and her cousin Jane picked me up and brought me back to the farm."

Patty rounded on him. "You met that girl last week?"

Walt stopped. "Yeah, why?"

"Not every girl shows up at a family funeral for a second look.

Unless you were slipping out at night to meet her after Thanksgiving?"

"Patty." They'd eaten the holiday meal around the kitchen table, too sad and tired to put much into it.

Patty clicked her tongue. "You're a goner."

"Uncle Walt! Look!" Alex, six, came barreling back to them, holding a robin's nest in his mittened hands.

"Hold onto that," Patty said. "They're good luck in a Christmas tree, and your uncle's going to need it."

Walt shook his head, but he didn't argue. Patty started walking again, but stopped after a few steps to turn back to him. "Invite her over to trim the tree."

He didn't have the heart to tell his sister that Molly Sanders was probably back at her college in Saratoga Springs, and not likely to waste much more time on a homebody like him.

Molly dialed the number inked on an empty page in her composition notebook. The payphone cord was too short to sit down on the industrial carpeting, so she leaned against the wall with the receiver tucked between her shoulder and her ear, tapping the page with her pen while it rang.

She'd looked the farm's number up in the phone book in her parents' kitchen before heading back to school, and there it stayed through the week's classes. The more days passed, the more she doubted herself. After one brief car ride and an awkward exchange at his father's funeral, what was the likelihood he was still thinking about her?

"Fuller Dairy." The voice on the other end of the line was the same soft, gruff delivery she'd liked so much three weeks before.

"Walt?"

There was a tentative pause before he responded. "This is Walter."

Molly's pulse jumped; he was adorably serious. "It's Molly Sanders. From Thornton. I'm glad you picked up."

"Molly? Oh, hey."

She was glad he couldn't see the fiery blush on her cheeks. "Forgot me so soon?"

"No, I…" He cleared his throat. "I didn't expect you to call, is all."

Molly inhaled deeply and went for convincing. Walt didn't have to know that she would stay in Saratoga Springs if he said no. "It looks like I'm going to be home this weekend, and I wondered if you wanted to hang out on Saturday, maybe I could make you dinner?"

"Well, I—" His voice dropped away so suddenly Molly was sure he'd hung up. "My sister bullied me into getting a Christmas tree. Maybe you could help me decorate it?"

Molly sucked in a breath, then clapped her hand over her mouth to suppress a giggle. Her roommate walked by, giving her a curious glance. Molly flipped open her notebook and silently pointed to Walt's number. Laura grinned and continued on to their room.

"I'd love to. I'll borrow my dad's station wagon. What's a good time?"

"How 'bout six? Murph and I can get the herd settled, and…" He chuckled. "You didn't call me to talk about cows."

A metallic voice informed them that Molly needed to insert another coin.

"I've gotta go. I'll see you Saturday at six." Molly hung up the phone and sagged back against the wall again. She hugged the notebook to her chest and closed her eyes for a moment.

After a moment, she dug into her pockets for another coin. She was going to need Jane to come down and spring her.

Saturdays meant Murph's day off. Walt hadn't thought about that in the heady rush of Molly Sanders' call, which was how he found himself driving into the village mid-afternoon to drop off his cousin Rosie.

She hopped out of the truck with a wave, brandishing her wages for a morning's work with the herd. "Thank for the ride, Walt. And the cash."

Thornton was dressed up for Christmas, garlanded and ribboned, piled with two storms' worth of snow. He hadn't given much thought to the holiday. Despite Patty's insistence that he get a tree, it was easier, out in the quiet valley, to shove aside the idea of Christmas Eve without his parents. Years of carol singing while his Pop played his fiddle, of recitations of *'A Visit from St. Nicholas* by the youngest reader —a position Walt had been happy to cede to Patty's kids a few years back—erased in one shattering morning. His family had fallen apart, and Walt wasn't sure where he'd fit when it put itself back together again.

The tree he'd cut was out in the barn in a bucket of water. Waiting for Molly's arrival.

Walt pulled the truck over and got out, leaving the keys in it. The river was half frozen, singing under the ice and warbling over the falls. The window display at the Ben Franklin wished him a Merry Christmas, the cheery bell inside the door welcomed him. Three steps inside the store, he found a pyramid of outdoor lights.

Flo, who worked the register, insisted on a paper bag for his purchases, and a candy cane for his pocket, as though he were still the child who'd come in for a candy bar on Sundays after church. He was still shaking his head when he very nearly collided with Molly on the sidewalk outside.

"Walt!" Her smile was dazzling. "Hey."

"Morning." *Morning?* Walt took a breath and started again. "Hi, Molly."

"How are you?"

It was a question he'd heard from everyone who'd spoken to him since his father's passing, one he'd responded to with an, "Okay, I guess," to deflect actual consideration of how he felt. He figured most people didn't really want to know. Somehow, from Molly's lips the words didn't seem like a pleasantry. It didn't seem to matter that he barely knew this girl at all.

"Been better, but I'm looking forward to seeing you later."

"I can't imagine," she said, sympathy shining in her eyes. "But I'm looking forward to it, too."

They stood on the sidewalk in the clear December sunlight for four heartbeats—Walt counted them as they thundered in his chest—before Molly laughed.

"I have to get home. I promised my mom I'd pick up a few things while I was in town."

"Oh, sure," Walt said. His hand in his pocket crinkled the wrapping of the candy cane. "Do you like candy canes?"

Molly's head tilted curiously. "Yeah."

He produced the candy cane in his palm, feeling suddenly foolish. He really had no idea what he was doing.

"You're sweet." She took the cane from his palm; maybe he imagined her chilly fingers lingering there a moment.

He'd missed casual affection in the last couple of weeks. He did okay on his own, but his parents had been—his mother still was—an affectionate woman. Molly had just crossed the street and Walt drank in the way she looked, the icy spray from the falls billowing up behind her as she crossed the bridge.

"Molly!" She stopped, turning back. "Let me walk you to your car."

Walt jogged across Main Street to join her.

"You don't have to. I'm just parked there by the library." She shifted the bag she was was carrying to her other arm. "But I won't say no."

Walt shrugged and fell into step with her for less than half a block.

"This is me," she said, stopping in front of a parked station wagon. They shuffled the bags between the two of them getting the doors open. Walt closed the car door for her, but not before he noticed a stack of travel guides stacked up on the seat.

He wondered how soon she was leaving. He imagined her with a crew of college kids like herself, shuffling on and off trains with huge packs and tourist maps.

She touched his arm, drawing him out of his reverie. "See you around six."

❧

Molly checked the laundry hamper twice before she loaded it into her dad's station wagon. A carton of raw cranberries, a paper bag of popcorn, thread and needle pinched from her mom's sewing box, some bittersweet and holly from the wild tangle of shrubs on their property line, and a Bing Crosby Christmas record. Molly wasn't sure how Walt felt about music, but you couldn't go wrong with Bing Crosby.

The moon was a low, snow-white crescent in a deep sky over the valley as she drove west out of town. Darkness came early in December, but the radio station out of Plattsburg was playing Christmas carols, and Molly sang along with enough gusto to hide her lackluster singing voice—and her twanging nerves.

It was five-fifty-five on the dot when she turned into the driveway at the Fuller's farm. The dairy barn hulked in its own shadow, and the pastures rolled away into the night, a study in lonesome moonlight and snow. The house, in contrast, was lit up from within with a warm, steady light that brought an involuntary smile to her face. She stopped the car on the gravel and cut the headlights—just in time to realize Walt was up a ladder, leaning into the front gable, long cords of colored lights dangling from the ladder and a hammer slung from his hammer loop.

"Be right down," he hollered.

Molly stood in the driveway, arms wrapped around her chest against the cold, while Walt put a nail in the peak of the gable, and hauled the lights into place along the roofline.

He climbed down, leaving the ladder in place, and crossed the front yard, chafing his gloved hands together. "Want to help me light it up?"

"Yeah."

He led her to the outlet on the outside of the wall, tucked behind a rhododendron in the front garden and handed her the plug. She wondered if he felt the zing of an altogether different kind of electricity when her mittened fingers touched his bare ones.

The lights brought the house to cheerful life, and Molly clapped. "It looks great."

"So," Walt said, face alight with pleasure, "what's the big surprise?"

"We're going to make a popcorn garland for your tree."

Walt carried her laundry hamper of supplies inside. Molly followed, shucking her coat and shoes by the door. Walt glanced at her sock feet.

Molly wiggled her rag-toe. "Keeps the dirt out. I might be a messy packer, but I hate dirty floors."

He was a tidy bachelor, she thought, but whether that was due to natural inclination or lack of opportunity to make a mess, she couldn't be sure. The wood stove was going in the parlor, and Walt set her basket down by the sofa. "I don't have much, but I've got some Schaefer in the fridge."

Molly opened the gingham tablecloth she'd wrapped around her offerings. "That's not very festive. I brought hot chocolate." She pulled out a large green Thermos, set it down on the coffee table, then dug back into the basket. After a brief search, she brandished a fifth of peppermint schnapps. "With a kick."

"You've got a regular picnic in there," Walt remarked, looking over her shoulder at the cranberries, the popcorn, and a foil-wrapped baking dish. "Is that a lasagne?"

"It's my specialty." Molly pulled out the popcorn and cranberries, then tucked the tablecloth around the dish. "It just needs to warm up. We can put it in when we get hungry."

"Molly?"

"Or I can put it in now." She pulled back one corner of the cloth.

"Molly."

Walt's voice had gone hoarse. In the same motion she turned and began to stand while he clasped her arm and tugged. She stumbled into his embrace. He wasn't too tall; she liked where she fit into his body. "I'd really like to kiss you."

His arms snugged around her and she rested her forehead against his nose, their breath mingling. "You definitely should."

As first kisses went, Molly thought, it wasn't so bad. If their teeth clinked and she giggled, if she wasn't sure what to do with her hands, it didn't matter. He tasted like mint, and when she didn't shy away, his lips slanted against hers, and the oxygen in the room went hot.

They kissed, openmouthed, unbothered by awkward hands, for a brief eternity. Full darkness filled in the shadows around the farmhouse, leaving them cocooned in warmth and light.

Molly caught her breath before it whooshed out in a nervous laugh. "We should heat up that lasagne."

Walt pushed his hands into his pockets. "How 'bout I go bring in the tree and the stand?"

Walt had no idea how to dress for a bonfire at Randy Strickland's parents' farm, but he'd missed Molly enough during her remaining weeks in Saratoga Springs to say yes to going with her before thinking it all the way through. He knew Randy and his older sister Charlene; farm families were like that. Randy was a few years younger than he was, enough so they hadn't been in school together. The Stricklands had a few dairy cows, goats, pigs, and chickens, but their main enterprise was found in acres and acres of Liberty and Northern Spy apples.

He zipped a sweatshirt over a Thornton Union High School t-shirt and laced up his cleanest pair of work boots, hoping they was the right thing to wear to a bonfire with Molly Sanders. By the time he made it out to his truck, he was glad of the parka, hat, and mittens he'd grabbed on the way out the door.

As he drove away, Walt realized he hadn't left the farm—or interacted with anyone save Murph, the farmhand who was nearly as old as his father—in three days.

As old as his father *had been*.

The mental correction caught in his throat. Generally, he'd been content to get up early with the herd, see to their needs, spend the day marking off the never ending list of chores the farm required, but he missed his Pop.

Anxiety rode shotgun on the drive south through town. *What if he was making more of Molly's payphone calls from her dorm? What if he was making too much of kisses and bonfires and a lightness that warmed his grieving heart?*

Molly Sanders was sitting on her parents' front porch steps in the same bell-bottom jeans she'd been wearing the day they met. He noted boots and her pompom hat. Down vest, wool sweater, scarf. Desire shot through him, burning away the jitters. Before Molly, he'd dated a couple of girls in high school, but the farm was a demanding mistress. What this girl did to his insides was new.

She stood when he eased the truck in behind the Ford station wagon he now knew to be her father's. He liked the way her body filled out the ski sweater and vest, but more he liked her wide, easy smile, the dusting of freckles on her nose, and the laughter in her eyes.

"You're on time," she said as he jumped down from the truck cab to meet her.

The darkness outside the pool of light from a lamp over the Sanders' garage was deep and cold. Walt could have stayed in that amber-white puddle of light forever, but his date had other ideas. She stretched up and kissed his cheek. "I like on time."

He led her to the truck, and Molly Sanders climbed into the passenger seat like she'd been doing it all her life. He closed her door, and took the long way behind the truck bed, stopping to consider the way the flat flood light through the windshield turned her cinnamon curls into a halo.

His sister was right. He was a goner.

He didn't say much, but Molly watched the way his smile played coy with his face when he snuck glances at her. Walt Fuller's eyes might be windows to an old soul, but the fireflies in her belly flocked to the light that flickered in them when he got out of his truck in the dooryard.

"See that break in the fence ahead?" she said. "Take that. Randy said we're meeting up at the mill."

Walt nodded, slowing the truck and turning onto the dirt road. They bumped down the frost-heaved tractor road that wound from Route 7 around the orchards to the abandoned mill, Molly wondering if he was thinking about the crackling atmosphere between them. Once the tidy rows of bare trees were behind them, she could see the glow of the bonfire through the woods beyond. A scattering of vehicles met them around a bend, and Walt stopped the truck.

He let out a long breath and pulled the key from the ignition. Molly touched his shoulder.

"Come on, let's go."

She paused for a beat when he let himself out of the truck. He'd surprised her, closing her door in her parents' driveway; she wondered if he'd come around to get the door for her.

Her patience was rewarded. Walt opened the passenger door and offered her a hand. With her feet firmly on the ground, Molly looped her arm through his and led him towards the fire pit.

A chorus of greeting rose up from the knot of people around the already blazing fire. Molly felt Walt hesitate and squeezed his arm.

"Walt! Hey, man." Randy Strickland got up from the log he'd been perched on. "Hey, Molls."

"Hi, Randy. Thanks for the invite. Nice night for it."

"Cold night for it." Walt reached out a hand, the two men shook hands. "Been a while."

"Yeah," Randy laughed. "Think the last time I saw you, we were out at your place for a party. Summertime?"

"My mom's fiftieth." Walt filled in the information.

Randy's grin sank. "Sorry about your old man. My folks didn't mention it until I got back from school."

"Thanks."

Molly snugged his arm against her to ward off the sadness she knew kept him company.

"There's beer in the cooler over there." Randy gestured at the circle around the fire. "Grab a seat."

A girl with a wheat colored braid hanging down over one shoulder was playing a guitar and singing, with help from a couple nearby. There was space on a picnic table across the clearing.

Molly slid her hand along his arm, twining their fingers where they met. "Want to grab a couple of beers? I'll grab some seats."

Walt nodded, and made his way to the cooler on the tailgate of another pickup. He met her at the picnic table with two bottles of Labatt's. Molly leaned against him when he sat, enjoying the way her head fit in the crook of his shoulder.

More cars and trucks filled in the makeshift parking, and the crowd around the fire grew. Someone left their car running, providing more music when the guitar-playing girl's fingers got too cold.

Cora Atkinson and her tall, dark-haired date joined them. "Molly! I didn't know you'd be here. You know John, right?"

"Hey, John," Molly said. "John Pease, Walt Fuller."

Walt's posture shifted, she felt him relax. "We know each other."

"Just a bit." John dropped down next to Walt with an easy grin. "How's the farm?"

Cora sat on Molly's other side. "John's parents live next door to the Cartwrights."

Molly tilted her head, squinting at her friend.

"Walt's Aunt Yolie?" Cora prompted her. "Walt's mom moved in with her sister after Jed Fuller died."

Cora went on, but Molly wasn't listening. Next to her, Walt was deep in conversation with Cora's boyfriend, more at ease than she'd seen seen him yet. His father hadn't been gone a month, his mother had decamped to her sister's—she knew from Janey that his sister and brother weren't nearby.

No wonder he was so solemn, with only cows for company.

She leaned into him a little more, the layers of clothing between them warming from the contact. In wordless answer, Walt's hand pressed against hers. A quiet gesture, but Molly's heart felt it just the same.

～

John Pease turned up at the farm three days later, dressed in flannel, denim, and work boots. Walt heard footsteps down the barn's wide center floor and stuck his head out of a stall he'd been clearing out.

"Walt?"

"Hey, John. C'mon back."

"What's goin' on?"

"Murph's out in the east pasture bringing one of the girls back. Doc Sutton is stopping by later to take a look at her."

John leaned against the stall's half-wall. "Do I want to know?"

"How'd'you feel about udders?"

"Bovine?" John grinned. "Not so much."

Walt chuckled. "You here to work?"

"If you can put me to use." John cast around the barn as if looking for inspiration.

"I'm walking the fence line by the Swift's place this afternoon. I wouldn't say no to company and an extra pair of hands."

"Sounds great."

Murph came around the side of barn door, leading one of the dairy's sweet-faced Brown Swiss. They were his mother's favorites— gentle girls with furry ears his mother loved to stroke as she crooned over them. His mom hadn't been back once since the day after the funeral, when his cousins George and Charlie had come by to help move her things to Aunt Yolie's house.

He ought to insist she and Aunt Yolie come out to the farm for Sunday dinner.

Who would cook dinner? He was pretty competent at the grill, but he'd stocked the freezer with an embarrassment of TV dinners since his mom left. He couldn't make a turkey or a ham to save his life.

Who would eat it, anyway? His Pop's had been the biggest appetite. For everything.

Molly and her lasagna flooded his thoughts. *Slow down there, Fuller.*

"Walt?" John was watching him, a mixture of pity and concern in his eyes.

Walt blinked. "Sorry, thinking about the vet bill."

"Bullshit." John's tone was conversational. "I wish you were thinking about Molly Sanders, not something that makes you look like a kicked dog."

John's uncanny question caught Walt off guard. "What about her?"

"She's pretty, and she likes you."

His friend's words unleashed butterflies in his gut. "Is that your law degree talking?"

"That's my eyes talking." John clapped Walt on the shoulder. "I don't get my law degree until spring. You like her, too, if I still know you. Let's take a walk and you can tell me what that's about."

"I wouldn't have figured Walt Fuller for a good kisser," Jane said. She was paging through the Sears catalog, and held up a page for Molly's approval. "Do you think something like this would be a good traveling suit for the honeymoon?"

"Does Bobby know you're planning that already?" Molly gave the camel-colored blazer and tailored trousers a once over. "You'd look good in that sweater or the striped shirt, but this is all winter stuff. You're going to want a summer suit if you get married in June."

Jane flipped the whole catalog shut with a quick huff. "You're right."

"Once we got out of our own way, he's a great kisser." Molly figured she was as close to an expert as anyone on that subject. They'd strung popcorn and cranberries while dinner warmed up. They'd kissed in the kitchen while the lasagne cooled. Walt brought down his mother's box of ornaments and tinsel. Molly held a crocheted sprig of mistletoe over his head, and they'd tangled together in a breathless heap on the plaid sofa cushions.

In the amber-dappled light of the Christmas tree, they'd snuggled front of the wood stove, drinking spiked hot chocolate and talking late into the night.

Jane was looking at her, having abandoned her trousseau shopping. "What about backpacking? Rome? Vienna? Athens?"

Molly wrapped her arms around her knees. "What about them?"

"You've been talking about going to Europe ever since you had to take that semester off for your gall bladder surgery, and your graduation got pushed back. Are you going to just give that up because Walt Fuller's more interesting than he looks?"

"That's mean." He was, though. Much more interesting, though Molly liked his looks just fine. "And a dinner date and some kissing doesn't mean we're getting married."

Jane's eyebrows rose, their groomed arches displaying her skepticism. "A dinner date you invited yourself on, *and* the bonfire at Randy's…" Her lips pursed just slightly as she trailed off. "I ran into Cora at the Rexall."

Molly laughed. "Okay, fine. I like him a lot, but that doesn't mean I have to give up Europe." Molly flopped back on Jane's bed. "It's not like I have the money to go, anyway."

"Well, the Fuller dairy herd isn't going to pay for it, that's for sure."

"Jane!" Molly sat up. Jane had paged past the suits and on to winter outerwear.

"Walt's already married to the cows, as far as I can tell, so I don't think he's headed off to backpack across Austria for a summer."

"You're awful." Molly lobbed a throw pillow at her cousin, who caught it neatly and set it on the foot of the bed.

Jane gave her the eyebrows again. "I'm practical. It's different."

Christmas morning dawned much like any other snowy winter morning. Walt rose before the sun, meeting Murph, who waited in his idling truck, two styrofoam cups of coffee steaming on the dashboard. By the time the herd was milked and pastured, the sun was up, and Walt's belly knew it was past time for breakfast.

Murph headed out. He had a sister down on Lake Bomoseen who filled a stocking for him.

Walt packed up his mother's picnic basket with raw milk for Aunt Yolie, and the best of the cuts from his beef share for his mother and the Cartwright cousins. His Pop had sold a bull calf the year before, knocking a fair amount off the sale price in exchange for the future meat. It wasn't much of a Christmas gift, but he hoped his family would forgive him. He'd spent most of his spare cash on gifts for Molly.

The Neil Young record was one he was gambling she didn't have already, since it was nothing new, just something that reminded him of her.

The small box weighed like a stone in his pocket.

Molly had invited him to join the Sanders family for pie and coffee after Christmas dinner; the idea of giving her a present in front of her parents and her little brother was something close to terrifying, but he'd seen the little opal egg on a slim gold chain through the window at the Mercantile, and known it would look beautiful around her neck.

Aunt Yolie answered her door, sweeping open the grand front entry—Walt both loved and feared his aunt's formal Victorian home. Eolia Cartwright was well into her seventies, but to Walt she'd always seemed old. She wore her steel gray hair in the same severe up-do he knew from his own christening photographs.

"Walter," she said. She was always formal, but there was kindness in her eyes. "Merry Christmas."

"Merry Christmas, Aunt Yolie." He leaned over the threshold to kiss her papery cheek, then followed her into the front parlor. His mother sat in a stiff wing chair, looking at—but Walt suspected not seeing—Yolie's Christmas tree. "Merry Christmas, Ma."

Tory Fuller was fifteen years her sister's junior, but you couldn't see it in his mother's grief-ravaged face. She'd paled since Thanksgiving, he noticed. Her gaze drifted toward him. "Oh, Walt honey. It's nice to see you."

Yolie fussed over him, putting the food from the basket into her fridge and ladling him a glass of thick, stingingly boozy eggnog. "She'll perk up when your cousins get here."

His mother did, in fact, perk up when the Cartwrights arrived. His cousins Charlie and George arrived with their families within moments of another. Between them there were six kids, and their happy noise filled the house.

George's wife Ginny paused near his position in the living room doorway, where he watched the littlest cousins opening their gifts. She stretched up to kiss his cheek, flicking a glance at the mistletoe ball Yolie always hung there. "You're quiet today. Even for you."

Privately, Walt had always considered Ginny Cartwright the most beautiful woman alive, even if she was a quarter of a century older than he was. Looking into her concerned eyes, he was defenseless. "I'm worried about Ma."

"She'll be okay. Losing the love of your life takes a lot out of you." She laid a hand on his cheek and smiled. "I heard you were spending time with someone."

"Word travels fast," Walt muttered, but he couldn't help the way his lips curved toward a smile. "Molly Sanders."

"I know her. She passed through my classroom a few times over the years. And George wrote her a college recommendation. She's a good girl."

"I know." He was having a hard time not letting his imagination run away with the future. Since the bonfire, they'd seen one another almost daily. Molly seemed content to visit the farm, and unafraid to pitch in, especially if it meant Walt had extra time to show her the secret places on the property. Just two days before, he'd taken her down to Fuller Creek, to the spot his Pop had put up the tire swing the summer he and Joe begged for one.

One the way home, they'd checked on the girls, and Walt had quite nearly confessed his love when Molly laid her cheek on the forehead of one of the Brown Swiss. She'd smiled at him over the cow's nose. "They're wonderful," she'd sighed.

So are you...

"What did you get her?" Ginny was watching him over her eggnog, while Charlie's twins squealed over new doll clothes.

"A necklace," Walt mumbled.

"I'm sure she'll love it." Ginny rested her head briefly on Walt's shoulder before going to see what her daughter Rosie was holding up.

Walt hoped so.

~

Molly's brother Eddie slept later than anyone that Christmas. By the time his sleep-tousled sixteen-year-old self came downstairs, the rest of the Sanders family was deep into their coffee and Christmas Kringle. They unpacked their stockings and opened a their gifts while the morning stretched out, stopping for bacon and eggs halfway through.

"When's your boyyyyyyyfriend coming over, Moll?" Eddie taunted, wearing his new ski jacket and a pair of mustard-yellow and brown striped hand knit socks with his sweats and Thornton High football jersey.

"Shut up, Eddie." Molly tossed a ball of wrapping paper at her brother.

"Language," Mrs. Sanders said idly, flipping through the cookbook Eddie had given her. Eddie and Molly rolled their eyes.

Her dad got up and rustled under the tree, producing a wrapped package the size of a department store shirt box and handing it to Molly. "Since your brother unwrapped his ski jacket and knows what he's getting for his big gift, it's your turn."

The box was light and a gentle shake revealed nothing. Molly unwrapped it carefully. Everything about this Christmas felt strange and magical. Inside, she peeled back folded tissue to reveal a plane ticket and a sheaf of museum pamphlets from European cities.

"Daddy? Mom?" She looked back and forth between her parents in disbelief. She'd never dreamed they'd give her the means to travel.

Her mom looked up. "You've worked so hard, honey, and we knew this was what you wanted most. Granny and Grampa Simon chipped in, too, and we got a good deal on the tickets from Simon's son who's a travel agent in Boston."

Molly barely heard her mother. She was looking at the round trip tickets to Paris, nine weeks apart. She was leaving on January 14th. "I'm leaving in three weeks?"

"We knew you were torn about working for one more summer at the camp." Her dad beamed. "Now you can do both."

Her mother leaned forward. "There's a check in there, too. Belated graduation gift from all your aunts and uncles on both sides."

Her gratitude clogged her throat. It was too much. *It was too soon.* Tears welled up in her eyes, and her parents faces crumpled.

"What is it, Moll?" Her father's voice was thick with concern.

Eddie lobbed the ball of wrapping paper at the kitchen wastebasket, sinking it. "She's just worried her new boyfriend's going to find someone prettier while she's gone."

"Shut up, Eddie!" Her voice cracked on a sob, but the whole scene was cut short by the doorbell.

Molly salvaged as much of her dignity as possible and headed for the front door, where Walt stood, holding what looked like a record. and a small box wrapped in shiny red paper.

"Merry Christmas, Molly," he said.

Molly promptly burst into tears.

Walt could see, through the Sanders' front door, Molly's family gathered around the Christmas tree, staring at them. Molly's face was in her hands, her shoulders shook. He grabbed a coat from the coat tree just inside the front door, rapped it around her shoulders and pulled the door closed, leaving them alone on the cold front stoop.

"What happened?" He pulled her close, not knowing what else to offer her.

She buried her face in his chest and clung to his waist for a moment, but the shaking stopped. When she looked up at him, her eyes and nose were blotchy with crying.

"I got my Christmas present." She sniffled and wiped her eyes.

"That bad?" He couldn't help but smile.

She gave him a wobbly smile. "Amazing, actually. Just... unexpected."

His own gifts still weighed heavily in his free hand while the other held her. "I guess these aren't exactly amazing, but maybe unexpected?"

He brought the two packages between them, offering them to her.

"Yours is inside," she said, taking up the record, and slicing the paper. "Neil Young. You surprise me."

"I wore this one out at the end of high school." He reached up to touch the curling locks of auburn hair around her face. "The day you and Jane rescued me, that's what popped into my head: Cinnamon Girl."

Molly set down the album on the empty planter that stood guard at the front door and took his face in her hands. "That is the most romantic thing anyone has ever said to me."

Her lips were cold, but Walt didn't care.

"Now…" She took the smaller box and unwrapped it, handing him the paper. When she lifted the lid off, she looked up at him. "Walt, it's beautiful."

"Not as beautiful as you, Molly."

A pair of fresh tears welled up and rolled over her cheeks.

"Hey, there. Don't cry." He thumbed away one falling tear.

She took the necklace out and held it up between them. "Will you help me?"

Walt took the chain, and clumsily at best, fastened it around her neck.

Molly took his hand. "Come take a walk with me."

She shrugged into the coat, fished in one of its voluminous pockets to find a striped ski hat in Thornton High colors and a pair of leather driving gloves that dwarfed her hands. She tugged the hat around her ears. "You grabbed my dad's coat."

She led him around the corner of the yard, through a hedgerow and into the large lawn that surrounded the Riverbend Hotel. The Revolutionary War-era tavern was dark, its windows lit with electric candles. Molly skirted the empty fountain and formal garden, seeking out a gazebo that looked out over the lawn towards the Catmint River.

"Three semesters ago I had my gall bladder removed."

Walt blinked. That wasn't what he'd expected.

"It pushed back my graduation, and while I was recovering from the surgery, I started reading old travel guides my Grampa Simon brought for me."

The travel guides in her father's car came to mind.

"Ever since then, I've wanted to go to Europe, stay in hostels, eat street food, see all the art and palaces and cafés..." She took a deep breath. "I just knew that the world was out there waiting for me to find it."

The gold band around the opal egg at her throat winked, and Walt's heart sank like a stone to his gut.

"My whole family got together to give me the plane tickets and some spending money." She squeezed his hands. I leave in three weeks. I'll be gone 'til late March."

Her eyes were shining. She couldn't know how lovely she was, sitting there telling him she was leaving. The stone in his belly cracked open. Once she'd seen the wide world, she wouldn't want a hardscrabble dairy farm in her hometown. Once she'd tasted French wine, walked museums and parks with other explorers, kissed men who'd seen the world, she wouldn't want a man anchored to the eighty acres his family had farmed for generations.

"It's going to be amazing, Cinnamon Girl." He swallowed the hitch in his voice. "You're going to be amazing."

"Wait," Molly said. "This is the thing I've dreamt about for a year and a half, and when I realized it was coming true, I cried."

He started to speak, but she hushed him.

"My first thought was, 'It's too soon.'" She shifted to be closer to him. "I cried because I didn't want... I *don't* want to fly off and leave you. Not now when you're still hurting, not now while we're figuring this out. And there you were on my doorstep, and I had this crazy thought that I would cash it all in and stay here."

He shook his head. "No—"

"I know," she rushed on. "All those talks we had, all the time we've spent together this last month, and I've never even mentioned it… Have you ever had a dream so big you can't tell the one person you feel like you really should? Like, if you give it words, it'll fall apart?"

Oh, Molly… "Yeah."

"I know we only met a month ago, and I know it's selfish to ask you to wait until spring for me, but will you? Will you still be here in March when I get back?"

The blood was singing in his veins. Relief washed through him. "I'm not going anywhere."

She launched herself into his arms, kissing him hard, then leaned back breathlessly. "Come on, let's go introduce you to my folks. And Eddie." She grimaced. "I'm sorry in advance about Eddie."

He followed her back across the lawn, through the hedges, and across her yard. Introductions were a blur, and he found himself with a cup of coffee and a slice of pie, sitting in the Sanders' living room while Molly's family scattered to their own corners of the house.

She handed him a box from under the Christmas tree, wrapped and ribboned. "It's not as nice as your present."

Walt opened the box to find a pair of boiled wool slippers in a size far too small for his feet. When he looked up questioningly at Molly, she was grinning.

"House shoes for me to keep at the farm. Those floors get cold in the winters."

He set the box next to him, and got up to cross the room to her. "That's the most romantic thing anyone's ever given me."

Molly stood, wrapping her arms around him, close enough that she had to tilt her face up to look at him. "I'm going to have to work on that between now and when I go."

"Merry Christmas, Molly."

She touched her lips to his. "Merry Christmas, Walt."

⌒

CAMERON D. GARRIEPY

From the World of Thornton Vermont

FOOLISH THINGS

THORNTON, 1999

*A*nneliese's last thought, before the cold erased her mind, was that people in love did foolish things.

That third Saturday of April was mild, drenched in watercolor skies and the pregnant smell of green and waking earth — ideal, her cousin Joss had dared, for bridge jumping. He and Jack were going up after supper. Would she come?

Toes curled over the edge of the bridge, spring breeze teasing the stray locks of hair that escaped her thick, honey-blond braid, she had felt invincible. Launching into the twilight with Joss and Jack at her side, flying out over the freezing river hand in hand with Jack, she'd understood how it felt to soar.

The Catmint River flowed west down the mountain from a clear spring in the Gap, making its way to join the Thorn just east of town. The bridge in East Thornton spanned a wide, deep glacial basin where the land curved and leveled. It had been a favorite summer swimming hole for as long as anyone could remember, but only the young and daring jumped before the snow in the Gap was finished melting.

Anneliese broke the surface with a shrieking gasp. Her skin was on fire, her muscles screaming in protest from the cold. She'd lost Jack when they hit the water; now she sought him out while her body thrashed its way to the river bank where Joss was crawling out of the water toward their towels.

"Jack?" Her voice was shattered with cold, but she couldn't see any evidence of him in the dim of the pool.

A hand grasped hers, and Jack surfaced, shaking river water from his near-black hair and whooping with adrenaline. He opened his eyes and grinned.

"Tropical." His chattering teeth and goose-fleshed skin spoke otherwise. "Come on, Banana. Let's shake off on Joss."

Anneliese followed him as he struck out with smooth strokes toward the rocky shelf at the edge of the river. Joss waited with their towels, happily back in the faded jeans and brand new Thornton College sweatshirt that was his post-college-acceptance uniform.

"How do you do that?" Anneliese shrugged into a flannel shirt and sweatpants, wringing her braid out in her wet towel.

Joss laughed. "Jump in, come up, get the hell out. I'm not crazy enough to actually swim in there before Fourth of July."

Jack pulled three beers from his backpack, popped the tops, and passed them around. "To six more weeks."

"Six more weeks," Anneliese echoed, sipping slightly before setting the can down beside her. She didn't understand the allure.

"Six weeks left and my sister is bugging me not to make a big thing about the fact that Mike Christensen asked her to our prom." Jack drank deeply from the can and suppressed a belch.

"Maybe because you're taking Mike's twin sister?" Joss leaned back on his elbows.

"I'm so ready for a new pond." Jack swished the dregs from his can, shook it out and tossed it back in his backpack. "Jenna Christensen is the hottest girl in Thornton, but there's only so much field hockey and, 'What sorority will I pledge at Bucknell?' a guy can take."

Joss nearly snarfed his Natty Light.

Jack snagged Anneliese's mostly full beer from beside her leg. "I should've just asked you, Banana. At least I'd enjoy the company."

Joss punched Jack in the arm. "Don't be an ass. I'm sure my cousin has done far better than you in the prom date department."

Unwelcome heat rose up Anneliese's neck. In the darkest, most honest corner of her heart, she'd wished for Jack to ask her, even while she knew that he regarded her as something between a sister and bro. One third of a trio that had existed since they were kids, even if it had faded a little since high school began and her social currency hadn't matched Jack's.

As a result of that hidden longing, she'd avoided the topic of their impending prom, and now she had two weeks to find someone to go with.

She took a deep breath and put on her best haughty attitude. "A lady is entitled to her secrets."

"Well," Jack snorted. "She told me."

Anneliese tried to resist the shiny new issues of *Modern Bride* at the circulation desk. Her American History final wasn't going to take itself; that was why she'd holed up in the Thornton Public Library instead of hiking with her dad.

As to why she'd said no to a prom dress shopping trip in Burlington with Sarah and Michelle, that was just pouring salt on the paper cut.

But those glossy, fairytale pages taunted her. Not that she wanted to get married—yet—but the fantasy of it, the luxury and whimsy, the idea that every bride's dream could be realized, that kindled a glow in her heart.

Did she picture herself in an array of couture gowns, on tropical beaches, under summer gazebo roofs and in autumn blanketed meadows? Of course. And if the fantasy groom had Jack Pease's clever, devil-may-care eyes and outrageous bed head, that was another secret for her private heart.

F.D.R. and the New Deal just sounded like a band; the words in her notes swam in front of her eyes, but she buckled down. As Jack had said the night before: six more weeks.

Joss would spend the summer on the farm before moving into the white granite and ivy dorms at Thornton College. Jack would leave for Williams and come home with a different, beautiful girl on his arm at every break, and she would be working at the antique shop her parents owned in Vergennes for at least a year before there was enough money for a semester of Hospitality and Tourism courses at the Community College.

The reality of life-after-graduation sat like a lead ball in her belly. She left her American History notes on the table and gave into a hundred and fifty pages of Monique L'huillier gown ads and destination ceremony articles.

"Girls up here really do get married young."

Anneliese snapped the magazine shut, blushing scarlet. "We do not!"

"Hey, easy. Just kidding." The boy in front of her was dressed like a J. Crew model, and he spoke with a cultivated smoothness that had nothing to do with the brusque New England cadences she knew. "So, you're not getting married?"

She tucked *Modern Bride* back into its spot on the periodicals rack and tilted her head up to get a good look at the too-charming teaser. "I'm not. I'm studying for a history final."

I'm studying for a history final. This was why Jack Pease was never going to see her as a girl to be liked.

The boy glanced over his shoulder at her neglected textbooks and notes. "I'm about as invested in my four term papers as you are in that final." His gaze turned to the sunlight streaming in through the huge paned windows that faced the street. "Is there anywhere in this town with a decent slice?"

Slice? Anneliese wracked her brain for an answer, but she had nothing.

The boy laughed at her obvious puzzlement. "Pizza."

"Oh!" The blush was back, but she had to laugh with him at her own cluelessness. "Yeah, down the street, under the VFW hall. Fantastic Pizza."

"Want to get out of here, grab a couple of slices?"

Anneliese blinked.

He rocked on the heels of his shoes. "Chris Greene, newly arrived in Thornton. And you are?"

"Anneliese. Thompson. But you can call me…" Anything but Anna. He'd probably rhyme it with banana, just like Jack… "Liese." She looked at her pile of study material, the dust motes dancing in the spring sunshine, and an implausible boy asking her to get some pizza. She breathed in and squared her shoulders. "Let's go."

Out on the sidewalk, book bags over their shoulders, Anneliese couldn't help looking around to see if anyone noticed her walking with Chris Greene. She wondered aloud how new to town he was.

"Got here three days ago." He held one strap of his bag, and rested the other in pocket of his fleece. "You know that mill project across the river? My parents are the preservation architects. Or consultants. Or whatever crap they spin it as. They're here for two months, and instead of letting me finish out the year at the school I've been at since sixth grade, they rented a house and arranged for me to write papers and take a couple of absentee exams."

Anneliese looked up at him, squinting slightly against the sun. "That sucks."

His laugh was grim. "Yeah well, they promised me a new car when I graduate, so I figure I'll take the buy-off and hit the road for the rest of the summer. As long as I get to Stanford by the start of the semester, I figure I'm all good."

"Wow." Most of Anneliese's friends and classmates were lucky to save up for a used Subaru or a loaner from a sibling away at college, or maybe the spare keys to their parent's car. Her parents let her drive their cars on weekends; Joss drove one of the old farm trucks. Even Jack, whose parents were sending him to Williams with a car, was getting his mother's Volkswagen with ten years and a hundred thousand miles on it. It was easier to focus on his casual mention of Stanford. "Stanford University?"

"Yeah. I just have to plan out the drive, and once I'm on the West Coast, my parents can relocate themselves straight to hell."

"Ouch." Something about his tone unnerved her. She couldn't imagine being that angry with her own parents.

"Don't worry about them." He flashed his catalog smile at her as they rounded the corner at the VFW—complete with the ever-present *Tuesday Night Bingo!* sign.

He held the door for her, and the spicy, greasy aroma of cheap pizza wrapped them up like a blanket. "I'm buying, what do you want?"

Chris bought her a slice of Hawaiian with Ranch dressing to dip the crust, without comment. He was from Westchester County, an only child who'd traveled to Europe and Asia and the South Pacific with his parents. He'd attended a private day school since sixth grade, and would be swimming for Stanford come fall. He spoke about New York City with casual familiarity that belied his just-shy-of-eighteen years.

Four hours after leaving Chris to make her way back to the library to meet her mother, Anneliese's thoughts were still in a booth at Fantastic Pizza. Her mother's were on more practical matters.

"Anneliese, where are you?" Mrs. Thompson took the damp dishrag from Anneliese's daydreaming hands. "Are you all set for your history test?"

Anneliese blinked away guilt. She'd all but forgotten the exam. When she fell asleep over her notes in the small hours, she dreamed of swimming pools in California the color of Chris Greene's eyes.

Anneliese met Sarah at Michelle's locker after third period to discuss their humanities project. With finals nearly out of the way, they had a five-week group project to wrap up, and then Spree Week leading up to graduation.

"We'll talk business over lunch." Sarah reached into her bag for a magazine cutout. "Michelle found this in your size at the dress shop yesterday. We pooled together on it. What do you think?"

It was a spaghetti-strapped, dark purple a-line gown with silver and purple crystal beading on the bodice and layered chiffon on the skirt. It was perfect. Anneliese blinked back tears. She had the best friends in the whole world.

Michelle pointed to the dyed purple shoes on the model. "You can borrow my silver strappy shoes. My mom's getting me new ones to go with my dress."

"You guys, that's amazing, but…" Anneliese thought of Jack, probably being crowned Prom King with Queen Jenna at his side, and thought she might be sick.

Sarah cut her off. "You're going. It's 1999. You can go to prom without a boy."

"Or we will find you someone, since you claim not to like any of the boys at Thornton Union." Michelle took the cut out and folded it up to tuck in Anneliese's bag, and the three girls slipped into the stream of teenagers headed for the cafeteria.

Sarah stumbled a little when a group of kids spread out across the corridor, pushing Anneliese straight into Jack Pease.

Jack steadied her with the hand that wasn't casually slung over Jenna Christensen's shoulders. "Hey, Banana. Sorry about that."

As he vanished back into the current, Anneliese heard Jenna giggle. "You don't have to be nice to everyone, Jack."

She wished she hadn't heard Jack's reply: "It's not like Anneliese is a threat. Jeez."

Michelle linked arms with Anneliese, sympathy in her big brown eyes. "God, Jenna is such a bitch."

Anneliese stayed after school with Sarah and Michelle to research their project, then walked into town for choir practice at the Congregational Church. The light was starting to fade when practice let out, so she headed for the book shop on Main Street. Marian Muse, who owned the shop, was a friend of her mom's and would let her use the office phone to call home for a ride.

She was halfway around the town common when a Lexus sedan pulled up alongside her, and the driver's side window powered down.

"Liese?" Chris Greene was leaning out the window to flag her. "You need a ride somewhere?"

She considered saying no for a half second, but it would be more fun than loitering in Marian's shop for twenty minutes waiting for her dad to pull up in his pickup truck. "Can you bring me home?"

"Hop in." Chris reached over to push the door open for her, and she climbed in.

The seats were buttery leather the color of camel hair, and the wood grain dashboard shone. She recognized "Thong Song," even if Sisqo wasn't her favorite. Chris had the volume up, but he turned it down a little while she fastened her seatbelt.

"Which way?"

She pointed to the stop sign where Main Street met Route 7. "Take a left, then about two miles up on the right to get to my neighborhood." She slid her palm over the supple seat. "Nice car."

"It's my mom's, but it's not a bad ride." He pushed the car as they climbed the rise out of town. He caught her eyes in the rearview mirror. "How was your test?"

"It's over, and I'm pretty sure I didn't completely fail, so…"

"That's a victory in my book." He pressed a button on the dash and Christina Aguilera poured out of the speakers. "Bet she's more your speed?"

"I guess." She fidgeted with her bag strap. "It's probably pretty lame, but I like Sarah McLachlan a lot."

When he snuck a look at her, Anneliese was acutely aware of her jeans, tee, fleece, hiking boots uniform. He was probably used to girls who understood pop music and fashion trends.

"How are your term papers going?" She directed him down the road to the subdivision where her parents' split level was.

"I'll get them done." He slowed the car when she waved at the sidewalk about three houses down from her own. "After all, new wheels are a pretty decent motivator."

She gathered up her bag and pulled the door handle. Without the car and Christina's vocal acrobatics, she felt awkward alone with him. "Thanks for the ride."

"I've got the car again tomorrow. I was thinking about seeing The Matrix in Burlington. You wanna come?"

Her heart sank. "I can't. I've got a project to work on after school, and I have to be home right after. My parents need me to babysit my little brother."

"No problem. I'll see you around."

He idled at the curb until she turned up her walkway, then gunned the engine, tearing down her street like the Lexus was a sports car.

Her parents went out for dinner and Tuesday Night Bingo every other week with Joss's parents. Her mother and his were cousins and old friends. Nothing fancy, but it was a long-standing tradition, and ever since she'd been old enough, Anneliese had assumed the babysitting. She sent her brother to bed after an extra TV show, and cracked open her math homework. Even though the exam was on Friday, her teacher was still assigning crazy amounts of homework.

The doorbell surprised her. She left her books on the kitchen table and approached the front door, peering out the living room window to see who was on the steps.

Chris Greene. His mother's Lexus was parked on the curb.

The front porch light threw his chiseled features into shadow and picked up the blond highlights in his sandy hair. She opened the door with a shy smile.

"Hey. What are you doing here?"

"You said you were babysitting. I figured I'd surprise you." He was carrying a paper grocery bag from the co-op. "I brought ice cream."

Her father would pitch a fit if he knew she was about to do this. She glanced at the wall clock in the hall. She had two hours before they got home from bingo. "Come on in. You have to leave before my parents get home, though."

Chris answered her nervous pronouncement with a cocky grin. "I figured." He paged through her math book while she grabbed a couple of spoons. "Want some help with this?"

"I shouldn't." She said, coming back from the kitchen. "But I need it. Calculus makes about as much sense as ancient Greek to me."

It turned out Chris had a head for numbers. He guided her through her calculus homework without giving her the answers, and he made her laugh while he was doing it. She wasn't sure she'd be able to replicate his tutoring on her exam, but at least the numbers and symbols made a little more sense than usual.

Chris had edged in close to her while they were working on her calculus. He was warm, and he smelled like soap. She had no idea what to do. She was used to palling around with Joss and Jack, had been kissed before, but this kind of closeness with a boy her age was something new.

When he closed her book and kissed her, Anneliese knocked her notebook off the table in surprise.

"You're funny," he whispered against her mouth before kissing her again, this time parting her breathless lips with his.

One hand was on her knee, sliding up her thigh over her jeans. The other cupped the back of her head under her thick braid. His tongue was slightly foreign in her mouth, but Chris didn't slobber like Ben Katz had that one time. She let herself drift, let Chris lead her.

This was how people kissed in movies. How she'd always imagined kissing Jack would be. *Jack.* She pushed thoughts of Jack Pease down deep, away from the reality of Chris Greene and his improbable interest in her, but not before Chris sensed her distraction and pulled away.

"I don't think I've ever made out with a girl over a calculus book."

"Me neither. A boy, I mean." Would she ever stop blushing?

"You want to try it somewhere softer?" He looked back across the front hall, where the living room sofa suddenly seemed twice it's size.

Her stomach rolled a little with nerves and adrenaline, but she stood up, feeling the warmth of his regard slide over her. She followed him into the living room, hastily tugging the elastic from her braid and finger combing her hair out over her shoulder.

Chris picked up a waved lock of her hair and let it fall over her shoulder. "I like that look."

Then he slipped his arms around her waist and pressed his mouth to hers. She leaned into him, and he lowered them onto the couch, his hands finding their way under her tank top and flannel shirt. The sound she made when his hands met the soft skin of her stomach was one she'd never heard from her own lips.

She saw fireworks behind her eyelids when he skimmed her breasts with his palms, but was relieved when he didn't press things any farther.

In fact, promptly at quarter to ten, he pushed himself up and pushed her hair back from her face. "I should go. I don't want to get you in trouble."

She sat up and tugged her clothes back into place. "Yeah."

He bagged up the evidence of their ice cream while she put the spoons in the dishwasher. "You want to hang out this weekend? You can come over to my parents' place. They're never around. We can watch a movie or whatever."

"I'll have to see if it's okay with my mom and dad. They're pretty strict."

"Gotcha." He put a hand on the door handle, but kissed her one more time before opening it.

"Chris?" She spoke all in a rush, the sudden, crazy question on her tongue before she could take it back. "Want to come to my prom with me?"

He smiled at her, all perfect teeth and porch-lit beauty. "Sure."

"Oh my god!" Michelle squealed, earning a sharp look from the school librarian. She dropped her voice to a stage whisper. "You did not."

Anneliese checked around them. She didn't want the other students around them to hear.

Hers was a selective shyness. It was one thing, swimming in your skivvies with your cousin and his friend during a July hike, or jumping into the freezing Catmint on a Saturday night, those stolen hours were the adventures of a semi-secret club of three. She knew the guys didn't talk about it; they'd been hanging out together since they were kids.

Letting a guy you barely knew come over while your parents were out, making out on the couch—asking him to prom—those were things she didn't need people talking about.

Sarah got straight to the point. "He said yes?"

Anneliese nodded silently, feeling her cheeks flame, but she couldn't stop the smile that broke like sunshine across her face. "I owe you two, that purple dress is lucky."

"Best prom ever," declared Michelle.

"So you three aren't going?" Jenna Christensen appeared at Michelle's shoulder, smirking and flawless.

Michelle peered over her cat's eye glasses, her brows vanishing behind her blunt bangs. "Who lit the fuse on your tampon, Jenna?"

Jenna's companions giggled before Jenna's sharp look silenced them. She turned the look on Michelle before sashaying off, friends in tow. "Go screw, nerd girl."

Michelle doodled a pair of frightened eyes on her notes. "The emptiness in her brain is scary."

Sarah watched Jenna and her entourage complete their library cruise through. "Miche, she is going to go all Carrie on you at prom, and I don't want the blood on my dress."

Anneliese sighed. The girl-drama exhausted her. "I wish I knew why she hates us."

Michelle looked at her like she was a complete doofus. "Because Jack Pease, whom she has finally gotten her nasty claws into just in time to be his final hometown fling, secretly loooooooves you, and while she couldn't explain it without crayons and puppets, she's wicked jealous of you."

"He absolutely does not."

Sarah nodded. "And it confuses her that he's nice to you, because you don't try. You're all L.L.Bean married the Gap, and she wants to be the trashy Express mannequin. Miche and me, she just hates because the hate sustains her, like blood in a normal human."

Michelle high-fived Sarah over their project papers.

"We've always been friends," Anneliese protested. And he's not that nice to me anymore..."

"He likes you." Michelle looked to Sarah for confirmation. "Even if he doesn't realize it yet."

When they left the school building an hour later, Sarah was offering to ask her parents to drive Anneliese home, when Chris stepped out of his mother's car and leaned on the roof. "Hey, Liese."

"Hey." Anneliese bit her lip and looked around, glad that there weren't many people left at school so late.

Michelle cleared her throat. "*Liese?*"

"Oh, right. Chris, this is Sarah and Miche." Anneliese twisted her hands together. "Miche, Sarah, Chris Greene."

"Do you guys need rides home, too?" Chris gestured to the car. "I've got room and my dad's expense account for gas."

Sarah looked searchingly at Anneliese, who was trying to make sense of his presence there, before answering. "My mom's on her way to drive me and Miche... I was going to ask her to take Anneliese, too, but..."

Anneliese was drawn to the Lexus—and the boy who drove it—like a magnet. "I'll see you guys tomorrow."

Miche's lip curved in a sly half-smile. "See you tomorrow, Liese."

Once inside the car, awkwardness occupied the space between her and Chris. "Were you waiting for me?"

He gave her a guilty look. "Nothing better to do, and I like you."

It became a pattern over the next ten days. Chris would find out when Anneliese was getting out of school or her other activities, and he would meet her and drive her home. Sometimes they got pizza or went to the library, sometimes they drove around.

Sometimes they parked the Lexus in quiet places and kissed, exploring what skin they dared discover.

She confessed her desire to be a wedding planner, recalling his catching her with her nose buried in a bridal magazine. He didn't seem fazed by her yearning to see places beyond Thornton, Vermont, places beyond New England beaches and Boston.

She didn't tell him about Joss and Jack.

They planned his summer road trip, drawing on maps and making lists of corny tourist attractions. Anneliese daydreamed about joining him, riding shotgun across the country, seeing everything, sharing rooms, sharing beds.

Chris promised to send postcards.

He rented a tuxedo for her prom; Anneliese asked him to meet her at Sarah's house. She just didn't know how to explain him to her parents. He didn't seem to care that she didn't want him to meet her family yet, and he didn't offer to introduce her to his.

Why invite trouble, when the dream was ending in a matter of weeks?

And then, just like that, it was prom night. Her exams were over, their project was underway, and it was prom night.

A cloud of Bath & Body Works scents hung over Sarah's room, and Anneliese could barely see through the cloud of Paul Mitchell.

"Anna, you look amazing!" Miche whispered in awe.

Sarah's mom stepped back with a flourish, and Anneliese took in her reflection.

Her long, thick, straight hair had been wound and braided into an up-do worthy of Cinderella. The slim purple dress made her look taller, and the borrowed push-up bra was like nothing she'd ever worn before.

She threw her arms around her friend's mother. "Thank you!"

"I'll leave you three to put on the finishing touches."

"Sarah, she needs a quick pedi." Miche rooted through the top drawer of Sarah's dresser, and pulled out three bottles of Sally Hansen Insta-Dri. "Silver, purple, or green?"

Sarah didn't hesitate. "Green. We're glamming this girl up."

Sarah lived a few blocks from the Thornton Grand Hotel, whose ballroom hosted the prom, so they walked, thankful for the softness of May and a dry evening. Chris held her hand, and she let her bare arm brush the wool sleeve of his tuxedo jacket. He'd chosen a silver tie and vest, and found her silver roses to carry. She could smell them as they walked.

She knew people were staring at her—at Chris. He danced, he joked with Sarah and Michelle's dates. He did it all looking like a Hollywood version of a teenager at a prom, and—if only for the spring, he was hers.

Chris was in the bathroom when Jack came up behind her. "You look great, Banana."

She whirled on him. "Why can't you call me 'Anneliese,' or 'Anna?' Like everyone else does?"

"I'm not everyone else, Anneliese." He stressed the corrected name. "And you know it."

The room tilted or her knees wobbled. Jack leaned in close. She could smell something spicy and smoky on his breath. His closeness forced a nervous giggle.

He stepped back as if stung. "Or maybe I am."

Jack saw Jenna coming back from the mocktail bar at the same time she did.

He was too slow. Jenna joined him, clinging like a burr to his arm. Jenna's voice was saccharine. "Hey, Anneliese. Aren't you the little Cinderella?"

"Guess that makes me Prince Charming?" Chris's voice wrapped around her just as his arm did. He looked Jenna over, eyes glittering. "My kid sister wore that dress to her friend's bat mitzvah three years ago, but don't worry. You wear it better." He pushed his hands into his trouser pockets and nodded at Jack. "Later, dude."

He leaned in to whisper in Anneliese's ear. "Fuck them. Let's dance."

By the time Lonestar's "Amazed" played and the DJ announced the end of the dance, the fairy lights and tulle in the ballroom outshone the stars, and Chris Greene was the axis upon which Anneliese's world spun.

He held her, turning under the lights, while the song spoke the words her heart felt. "Where're we headed after?"

"After?" She'd figured they'd go out with everyone for late night diner food and then hang out at Sarah's if everyone wanted to stay up, but they'd never talked out it.

"Yeah. We could go back to my parents' place for a while. They're out of town this weekend, checking on another site."

The two of them alone. Her parents thought she was spending the night at Sarah's. It would be so easy.

Too easy.

"I can't." She leaned back in his arms to meet his eyes. "But I want to."

"Liese!" Chris was waiting for her after school as usual, but today he was perched on the back of the bench in front of the school instead of loitering in front of his mom's car.

Anneliese split off from Sarah, Miche, ignoring the slight eyeroll her friends exchanged.

Chris jumped down and slung an arm around her. "I got it!"

"Your diploma?" Anneliese dropped her bag and hugged him.

He was laughing. "No, they'll send that to my parents." He turned her around.

Parked in the fire line, top down, and gleaming black was a sleek roadster. Anneliese gasped. "Oh my god, it's gorgeous."

He hugged her to him. "Let's take it out to Chimney Point and over the bridge."

Anneliese glanced at the sky, heavy with spring rain, but dry for the moment. Chris's delight was all the sunshine they needed. "Let's go."

"Bana—Anna!" Jack's voice tugged her attention from Chris and the car.

She turned. Jack, with Joss at his side, was crossing the grass. "We're going to hike out to the Stone Garden, see if we can beat the rain. Wanna come?"

Jack rarely spoke to her in full sentences at school, never mind openly discussing their sometimes adventures in front of classmates. She blinked at him, not sure what to say until Chris's impatient hand pulled hers.

"Can't. I've gotta go."

The Audi growled along County Road, devouring the miles. Anneliese couldn't help laughing at the feeling of flying along familiar roads in such an alien way. Joss's parents' dairy was a blip on the map, the rolling hills and curves that textured the valley gave the Chris a chance to open up the engine and soar.

They crossed Lake Champlain and turned around at Crown Point to cross it again. The wind at the crest of the bridge was cold and scented with lake water. Anneliese breathed it in, trying to capture the freedom. It would be something to savor when she was inventorying antiques in Vergennes all winter.

When a shower threatened with a few drops on the windshield, Chris took them south into Shoreham, along a winding road through orchards and farms until they pulled up in front of a beautifully restored farmhouse. The rain chased them, cutting across the lake as they drove.

Anneliese was charmed. "Where are we?"

"The place we're renting." He was putting the top up just as the rain came, sheeting and sudden. "It's dry—and parent-free."

They made a run for it, dashing from the car to the breezeway.

There was a remote-controlled gas fireplace in the living room. Chris turned it on, and tossed the remote on the overstuffed sofa. "My mother didn't want the mess of a real one."

He pulled her down on the sofa with him and tugged the elastic from her braid. His hands were cold from driving, and rain clung to his hair. She shucked off the flannel shirt she'd been wearing.

"She wouldn't like me, would she? Your mother." Though the temporary home was devoid of any personal effects, Anneliese imagined she could feel Chris's parents disapproval in the comfortable, catalog furnishings.

"I don't think she likes me. Or my dad, for that matter. Not very much anyway." Chris snugged her up against his body. "Which is why I'm out of here, away from them, as soon as possible."

Anneliese tilted her chin to look at him. "I'm sorry." She didn't know if she was sorry he didn't feel loved or sorry he felt the need to get away. Or if she was sorry that he would leave her behind. Nothing tethered him to Thornton.

Chris chose another remote, and Sarah McLachlan crooned from hidden speakers. He touched her, and gooseflesh rose on her arms. She wanted him so badly, but she stilled his questing fingers when they slipped into the waistband of her jeans.

He contented himself with the skin of her back and the soft curve of her breasts, camisole pushed up, bra straps slipped aside. He shed his t-shirt, and Anneliese thrilled at the feel of their bellies pressed together on that borrowed sofa. The fire and the rain lulled them after a while, and it wasn't until the sharp report of the door woke them that Anneliese realized they'd fallen asleep in one another's arms.

There was a flurry of humiliated dressing when his parents appeared in the archway, and Anneliese slunk off to the powder room to hide her flaming cheeks, but she couldn't hide from Chris's parents' biting remarks.

...Small town nobody...

...God help you if you've gotten her pregnant...

...Ruin your life...

She steeled herself to leave the relative safety of the half-bath, but Chris's voice stopped her. There was a dangerous, cornered-animal growl in his voice that shocked her.

"Stop. Both of you. Just stop. She's nice. Smart and kind and she doesn't give a shit about you two or your house in Westchester or your flat in London or the beach house in Maine. She doesn't even know about any of it." He paused, and a leaden silence filled the heartbeat. "She likes me, and I'm going to take her home now. If the two of you could just go…somewhere else for five minutes so she doesn't have to look at you after the things you just said, that'd be good."

She turned the doorknob as silently as she could, but Chris wasn't finished.

"And she's the one who stopped things. So, no Mother, I haven't gotten her pregnant."

"Are you going to?" Sarah cut right to the core of it. "Sleep with him?"

The weeks since prom had been a sweet agony of wanting and fear, bliss and frustration in equal measure. The fight with Chris's parents lingered in the air between them, but he wouldn't bring it up.

He never pressured, but he'd made his desires completely clear. Anneliese was drunk on new love and fresh lust, a distracted tangle of hormones and confusion. They drove one another as near to the edge of no return as was possible.

An afternoon at home with the girls felt foreign and—if she was being honest—welcome.

"I don't know." The war between wanting and not knowing if it was the right thing to do was tearing her up. "He's leaving. He hasn't met my parents, and let's just say his aren't fans of me."

"You say he doesn't seem to be a big fan of his parents." Miche matter-of-factly licked the Phish Food from her spoon and passed the pint. "And yours would shit a brick if they knew how much time you've been spending with a boy like him."

"I don't know, Anna." Sarah took the ice cream. "He's really hot, but like you say, he's kind of passing through, and it's your first time…"

Michelle snickered. "He did defend you from Jenna at prom, though. He can't be all bad."

"He's not bad at all," Anneliese protested.

Sarah tsked. "Maybe not bad, but way too smooth."

"Who is?" Mrs. Thompson came upstairs with a basket of folded laundry and checked the time on the kitchen clock. "Just about time for you two to head home."

"Yes, Mrs. T." Sarah started to gather up their project materials. She handed out lists to Michelle and Anneliese. "Anna's going to get the report copied and bound. Miche, you've got the Power Point thing, and I'm going to write the oral. We've got this."

"Later, Anna." Miche dropped her dirty spoon in the sink, and grabbed her bag. "Bye, Mrs. Thompson."

"Is this about that boy you've been hanging around with?" Anneliese's mom took the pint of ice cream, capped it, and tucked it in the freezer. "The one you don't seem to think your dad and I deserve to meet?

Anneliese clutched the list in her fist. "How did you? I mean…"

"Molly saw you get into some black sports car with a boy driving. Understandably she wondered who he was." Mrs. Thompson snapped out a clean dishtowel and tucked it over the over door handle. "How long has this been going on?"

Anneliese felt her courage dry up on her tongue. "A month."

Mrs. Thompson leaned against the sink. Her disappointment was silent, heavy, and stinging. "You know the rules. You're not to see him again until your father and I have met him."

"Mom, I'm seventeen."

Her mother pushed away from the counter. "And you still live under our roof, and we expect you to behave like a lady. Have him come over when we're home, and we'll meet him. Until then, you don't see him, except at school."

Anneliese didn't correct her mother's assumption. One more lie wasn't going to hurt anyone.

Once she started lying outright, instead of just holding back the truth, Anneliese found it got easier.

The last Saturday before graduation, she asked her father for a ride to the library, feigning last minute project work. Chris picked her up as soon as her father's truck was gone.

They drove south to Arcadia Falls with a picnic blanket and a co-op sandwich feast.

Chris was unusually quiet while Anneliese led him deeper into the woods, up the hillside trail that would bring them to the peak of the falls. She knew the pools that formed like bowls in the rocky spillway would be chilly, but warm enough to dip feet into on a warm spring afternoon. With his time left in Thornton running out, she wanted to give him more to remember than someone else's prom, a rented house, and a small town library.

She wanted—she thought—to give him herself, but she lacked the words to tell him that. Here at Arcadia, one of the secret places she'd only shared with Joss and Jack, here was where she hoped she might find that last secret part of herself to open up to him.

She fussed with the picnic blanket, smoothing and pressing at the edges until it was just so. She arranged the prepared food three different ways before Chris broke the silence.

"Come with me."

Anneliese froze over the butcher paper-wrapped sandwiches. "What?"

Chris squatted down, resting his forearms on his knees. "Come with me. To California. You can get a job in a shop and work your way through college anywhere. You don't have stay here. Come with me. I have the car, I have a place waiting for me when I get to Stanford. I'll help you. We'll be together." He searched her eyes. "We can see the country together. We can do everything together."

The blanket seemed so much farther away, gravity failed to tether her to the ground. "Our families ..."

"Will deal with it." He dropped to his knees and pulled her close, kissing her. "Come with me. We'll be crazy and amazing together."

"Chris?" She took his face in her hands and looked for some clue that he was teasing. She found none of his almost arrogant confidence. "You mean it?"

"We'll do the trip we planned, but you'll be with me. We'll leave notes." He kissed her again, pulling her to her feet and swinging her around. His joy was boyish. "We'll go right after you graduate. I'll bring you back for Christmas. My parents won't care, and yours will have to forgive you when they realize how happy we are. It'll be great. I'm better with you."

"Yes." She nodded and kissed him back. "I'll go with you."

He swung her off her feet and held her tight.

The only sounds were those of the woods and the falls, but Anneliese felt the universe explode in her heart. He was right. She could do the things she wanted to do anywhere, and they could be everything together wherever they were. Their friends, their families, would forgive them.

People in love did foolish things.

CAMERON D. GARRIEPY

From the World of Thornton Vermont

PAST AND PENDING

Nan shifted the conversation away from herself and Joss. "We're here now, Kate, so why don't you tell us all why you're not back at that gallery seducing Seth."

Jack nearly choked on his beer. Kate took a long swallow from hers.

"He always acts like he's interested," she began, "but there's a Big Hurt behind his eyes." Jack and Joss exchanged a look. Nan wondered if Kate's assessment hit too close to the mark.

~Damselfly Inn

In matters of love loss, we've no recourse at all.

~Shins, *The Past and Pending*

CAMBRIDGE, MASSACHUSETTS

APRIL 2007

"Heads, you let me walk you home tonight; tails, you give me your number, and I call you in three days to ask you out."

Seth Weston popped the cap off a bottle of Red Stripe and presented it to the woman next to him at the bar.

She was alone and she was gorgeous – all loose brown curls and stormy eyes. He'd noticed her chatting with the bartender at the Phoenix for an hour or more, casually turning away every suitor who approached. Seth had no idea why he should have any more chance than a half-dozen other guys, but he'd have kicked himself later for not saying hello.

Astonishment, backlit with laughter, widened her gray-violet eyes. "It's a bottle cap, not a quarter, and you've got to be kidding."

"Fine. Smooth side down you let me call you sometime." He flipped the bottle cap; it landed smooth side down in his palm.

She squinted in mock resignation. "You win."

The tiny furrow between her eyes enchanted him. She set down her highball glass and grabbed the bartender's pen with a flourish. Cupping his hand in hers, she picked the bottle cap up from his palm and wrote her name across his lifeline followed by ten digits.

Seth read the upside-down writing. "Sara."

She rolled the bottle cap between deft fingers. "And you are?"

"Seth."

"And what do you do, Seth, when you're not badgering helpless females in Central Square bars?"

If she was a helpless female, he'd eat his Williams College hat. "I craft witty pick-up lines and work on my etchings."

She laughed out loud. "Of course you do." She sipped her drink and cocked her head to one side. "Really, though. What to do you do?"

With practiced smoothness, he flipped his wallet open and pulled out his business card.

"Right now, I'm managing a gallery on Newbury Street, but I'm thinking of taking on a few artists as an agent."

Sara looked at him and then at his card in her squinty, furrowed way. "Didn't make it as a... photographer?"

"Jesus." He was taken aback at her pinpoint accuracy. "Actually, yeah."

"You have that preppy-and-not-tortured-enough look about you."

Seth resisted the urge to look for some common friend of theirs standing behind him with a cue card. *How had she done that?* "We haven't met, have we? You're not just playing with me here?"

"No." She laughed at him, cheeks pink with amusement. "And though you haven't asked yet, I am currently spending my inheritance on a graduate degree in English Literature at Harvard and housesitting for my father while he lectures in Europe. He is the darling of physics nerds the world over. They flock to hear him speak wherever he goes." She giggled at Seth's stunned expression.

He was barely done reeling from her frank assessment. "That's... Intense."

"I know."

Time to ask, he was getting in too deep. "Are you meeting someone here?"

She took his beer from him, set it down on the bar next to her glass. "You, apparently. So, come on. You can walk me the mile back to my house."

She pressed her palm against the place where she'd scrawled her name, and led him from the room.

Out on the street, last calls were sending patrons pouring out onto Massachusetts Avenue. Still holding his hand, Sara tugged him to the left outside the bar. "Tell me about whatever you're working on right now."

"We've got an opening next week. A photographer from the Hudson River Valley, really stark black and white architectural images, and then a Japanese carver."

She fidgeted with the Red Stripe cap. "I don't get that stuff. I like Van Gogh, especially the cafe painting with all the golden light. I want to eat there, with the night sky and the light."

Seth almost suggested they leave for Marseille that very night. *How far could it really be from there to Arles?* But Sara guided them into the gracious warren of residential streets between Mount Auburn and Brattle, and he forgot the south of France.

She turned up the walkway to a cream and blue Georgian colonial. "This is it."

When she fell, it happened so quickly Seth didn't manage to catch her. Her impossibly high, dangerously narrow boot heels snagged in the mossy crag between two worn bricks and she toppled.

"Fuck! Ow!" She drew her hand up to her chest. He saw that she'd skinned her knuckles when she fell.

He crouched down, taking her by the elbow and helping her up. There were tears balanced on her lashes.

He brushed them away when they spilled down her cheeks. She opened her curled hand and the bottle cap fell to the bricks, revealing a cut in her palm, blood welling in the serrated curve.

"Well," she said, breathing deeply, "You have to come in now. I can't very well bandage my own right hand, after all."

Low light spilled out of an archway at the end of the front hall. Sara gestured to a door on the left. As he searched the closet for a coat hanger, she slung her own jacket over the curving railing that soared up along the stairway to the second storey and made her way along the hallway, flipping lights on as she went.

He wrestled a hanger from the closet rod and crammed his jacket in alongside the contents of every L.L. Bean outerwear catalog issued in a decade, before following the light towards his host.

Seth stepped into the kitchen and into an HGTV fantasy.

The kitchen was spacious, lavishly appointed, and spotlessly contemporary, without leaving behind the house's classic influence. Copper pans hung over a huge professional range, potted rosemary grew on the windowsill, a bowl of lemons rested on a butcher block island. The room opened out into a sunken great room with cathedral ceilings that pushed away from the main building into a garden lit only by moonlight and the amber glow of nearby streetlights.

Sara was banging around in a vast pantry. He could smell something toasting, and she'd set out two pint glasses with logos from local watering holes on them.

The toaster dinged, and Sara popped her head out of the pantry. "Can you grab a plate? I can't find the first aid kit."

Seth peered into the glass-front cabinets until he found a plate he wasn't terrified of smashing, and inspected the contents of the toaster.

Pop-Tarts.

With a chuckle, he snatched them from the hot toaster and dropped them onto the plate.

Sara emerged with a small first aid kit, flipped it open on the counter, and laid her hand, palm up, on the counter. "Patch me up. I'm hungry."

With Sara's hand salved and wrapped up, they took the Pop-Tarts, glasses and a heavy glass bottle of chocolate milk out through the great room into the deeply shadowed garden behind the house.

Sara eschewed the iron patio set and the quaint swinging bench under the wisteria arbor, and drew them both down on the damp lawn to share their midnight feast.

His butt was soaked through his jeans, his toes were cold in his

Cole Haan loafers, and he was more content than he'd been in a very long time.

Sara lay back on the damp grass. "Stars are especially pretty when you're a little drunk. When you're a little drunk and eating Pop-Tarts outside in April? That's when they look like Van Gogh stars." She patted the empty space beside her body. "It's just dew."

Seth reached across her legs to set his glass with hers on a paving stone path that wound through the property. Sara's hand slid up his other arm; her fingers stilled under his rolled up shirt cuffs.

He shifted his weight, and lay down beside her, staring up into the sky and letting his imagination conjure the swirling coronas she saw in the sky.

When once again her palm sought his, he thought of the ink on his skin and how it would blur like Van Gogh's starlight.

~

"Miss Sara!" The sliding door banged against its frame. "You will catch your death!"

Seth woke, stiff and cold, with wet grass clinging to his cheek, to blue skies and a watery spring sunrise. Sara propped herself up on one elbow and looked back at a plump woman with spiky fuchsia hair standing in the doorway, muttering to herself in a language Seth couldn't decipher.

"Birgit, I am not going to die from sleeping outside in April." She grinned at Seth. "He might, though. Will you make coffee?" She batted sooty lashes at the woman. "Please?"

Birgit swung herself around and muttered off—he hoped to make the coffee Sara had asked for.

"Morning, Sunshine." Sara pushed herself up to sitting and ran her fingers through her hair. "I didn't mean for it to be a sleepover, but it looks like we skipped ahead a bit. It's appallingly early. Breakfast?"

He let his eyes close, thankful he hadn't had too much the night before. He opened his eyes again, thankful Sara's face was still there. It would have been easy to believe he'd dreamed the whole thing.

"You're about the same size as my big brother. I'll get you something of his to put on. You're a mess."

There was nothing to do but follow her.

Inside, Birgit was measuring ground coffee into a complicated looking machine built into the wall. Sara went to her, laying her head on the woman's ample shoulder and squeezing her waist.

"Birgit, you are an angel. I'm going to get my friend here some clothes from Kip's closet. Be nice."

Seth offered the woman an awkward smile. "Seth Weston."

Birgit shrugged and pushed the filter basket into the coffee maker.

Seth slid the driest part of his rear end onto a barstool at the kitchen island and listened to the burbling of the brew cycle.

Seth walked home with a belly full of Scandinavian doughnuts. Birgit, he now knew, was Estonian, and drew from a vast well of Nordic and Eastern European cuisines and languages. She had been Sara's and her brother's nanny, and had stayed on as the housekeeper after their mother's death.

Sara talked through a trucker's breakfast, weaving him into the narrative of her family's adventures as snugly as if he'd been along for the ride. If she was serious, she'd also planned out the entire summer for them.

He caught his reflection in a secondhand clothing shop window. A mannequin in the window display wore a vintage babydoll dress and a motorcycle jacket, with a silver tinsel wig. She winked saucily at the passersby; he wondered if Sara had a jacket like that.

His Tulane tracksuit-clad body looked foreign to him, looking out at him from the plate glass. His borrowed clothes boasted Sara's brother's alma mater. He'd never even owned a track suit from his own.

"We should go," Sara had said over a third *ebelskiver*. "Unless you're a terrible traveler. Are you a terrible traveler? New Orleans in May; my god, Seth. Kip's boyfriend plays piano all over town. We can stay up all night singing, and have beignets when the sun comes up."

He'd only stopped by the Phoenix the night before to hear a band his boss recommended. Anything to get on the pretentious douchebag's good side, at least until he got a few clients of his own. He now suspected he'd found far more than a conversation starter.

Seth's phone rang, and he dug it out from the Whole Foods Market shopping bag that contained his damp clothes. His buddy Jack Pease's name flashed on the screen, and he pressed the answer key, wincing as an ambulance screamed by on the next block.

"Hey."

"You around?"

Seth could hear a siren echo back through the phone. "I'm in your neck of the woods, actually. Sounds like you are, too."

"You're in Cambridge? At nine AM on a Saturday? Are you working?"

Seth leaned against a railing overlooking the stairs to the Harvard Square T entrance. "It's a long story."

"You can tell me over overpriced beer and soggy hot dogs. I've got Sox tickets. Eleven-oh-five game."

Seth mapped it out in his head. He could make it home to change and still get to Kenmore Square before the first pitch. "I'll meet you outside the Cask."

Explaining Sara to Jack might help him figure out what had happened the night before.

This morning's world was a strange new place.

At the top of the eighth, Seth carried two beers past the knees of the eight people between the aisle and his seat. Handing them to Jack, he wedged himself into one of Fenway's narrow folding seats and adjusted the brim of his faded Sox hat.

Jack passed his beer back to him, leaning forward with his own to squint at the pitcher's mound. "You missed *America the Beautiful*, you communist."

Seth snorted. "'Purple mountains' majesty' or one last round?"

Jack tipped his cup against Seth's. "Cheers." After hollering his displeasure at the umpire, he turned to Seth. "The game's nearly over. You gonna tell me now about the ink on your hand and how you ended up in Harvard Square this morning?"

Sara's name and number were still just barely visible on his palm. The tenacious black ink had blurred and faded to indigo in the shower, but like thoughts of the woman herself, the brand stayed with him.

"I met a girl last night at the Phoenix. I slept in her backyard. Her housekeeper made me breakfast. I really want to see her again."

Jack shook his head and sighed. "Start at the beginning."

Seth told Jack the whole thing, except the stuff about Van Gogh, and the casual invitation to spend the summer traveling together. Jack had a player's instinct for staying out of tangled relationships. He'd see flags and hear bells a mile off.

"If it goes any further than breakfast pastry, we should go out next weekend." Jack stowed his empty cup near his feet, and sighed. "Rachel keeps telling me she wants to meet my friends."

Seth blinked at the unfamiliar name. "Rachel?"

"The hostess from Beast. Did I tell you about her?"

"Yeah, sorry. Forgot her name."

Jack shrugged. "Fair enough."

The Sox lost, but it was hard to take the loss too badly when the sun was shining and a spring breeze teased its way amongst the old ballpark's aisles. Seth's phone rang as they were making their way through the crowd on Yawkee Way.

Jack peered down at Seth's phone display.

Seth answered the call, elbowing Jack to get some space. Sara's voice was warm in his ear. "I'm sure you're still full of *ebelskiver*, but what would you say to sangria and tacos? I don't actually know where you live, but I'm on my way through Kenmore, and I'm jonesing for Mexican." She paused while a pack of mostly drunk Sox fans rambled by Seth, belting out *Sweet Caroline*. "I'm happy to get a head start on the sangria while I wait for you."

"I'm not far from there. Which place?"

Sara's destination was only four or five blocks away.

"I'll see you in a few."

Seth glanced apologetically at Jack, who was leaning against a pedestrian signal pole watching him with barely concealed amusement.

"I'm on my own, I take it?"

Seth grinned. He was already turning in Sara's direction. "Thanks for the game, man. Catch you later?"

Jack mock saluted. "Later."

Sara was nursing a hardcover book and a pint glass of garnet-colored sangria, and had already made her way through a basket of tortilla chips and guacamole when Seth found her at a sidewalk table in front of the taqueria.

She looked up from the pages only when his shadow fell over them.

"Hey."

"Thank god." She folded the dust jacket between her pages, and closed the book. "I was going to eat the pages if you didn't turn up. Salsa might just spice up the Pasternak enough to be palatable."

Doctor Zhivago, Seth noted. Not exactly light reading for an April afternoon. He dropped into the seat opposite her. "What brings you all the way over here?"

"Appointments of the boring variety." She scraped at the remains of the guacamole with a broken corner of chip. "I am nothing if not a woman about town."

He started to pick up the menu, but she held it to the table with a fingertip.

"Do you trust me?"

"If I didn't trust you, last night gets a whole lot weirder, huh?"

She laughed, catching the server's eye as she did. She handed the young man both folded menus as soon as he reached the table. "Ten tacos *al pastor*, and a pitcher of sangria with a fresh glass for the gentleman."

"What are we eating ten of?"

Sara leaned over the table. "Spit roasted pork, dripping with slow-cooked pineapple juice, some kind of magical green sauce, warm tortillas. Deliciousness."

"Ten of them?"

Her answering snort was the most endearing—and least ladylike -- sound he'd ever heard. "They're small. And if you don't order two more to go before we go back to my place," she tapped the bill of his Red Sox cap, "I'll eat your hat."

The casual mention of her place zinged through him. He concentrated on chips and guacamole for a moment to contain the lust it inspired, but flirting with her came as easily as breath. "Your place?"

Her smile was positively feral, complete with a slow lip-bite. "We're going to go old school for the second date. I want to make out with you in the rec room and listen to all my mopey high school CDs."

He considered her for a moment, doing the math and recalling what the girls were swooning over in those years. "Remind me to thank Mazzy Star someday."

She laughed out loud. "Especially if I let you get past first base."

MAY 2007

"Hey, artboy. When do you knock off?"

Seth looked up from a catalog layout mock-up for the gallery's next installation. Sara let the door fall shut behind her and skipped across the ultra-modern interior of the Newbury Street gallery.

"They're really fighting the mood of the neighborhood in here, aren't they?"

He chuckled. "Hi yourself. And it's all for the art."

She squinted at the bright white walls, polished floors, and carefully tracked lighting. "I prefer the Uffizi."

"We can't all have former Medici office spaces for our masterpieces." He closed the catalog galley, and walked around the desk to kiss her. Fatigue faintly smudged her eyelids. "You okay?"

"Fine." She turned to a collection of miniature statues on pedestals in the center of the room.

"Are you free this weekend?"

"We close in an hour, and I have no concrete plans until I'm back on the schedule on Tuesday."

Sara leaned down to inspect the tiny carvings. "What are they?"

"*Shunga netsuke* in agate. They're—"

Sara giggled. "They're sexy little things aren't they?"

Seth slid a hand up her bare arm. "They are. You smell good."

She leaned into him, just a fraction. "Chanel *Coco*, if you're looking to spoil me."

"So, what did you have in mind for the weekend?"

"Nothing quite this elaborate," she said, peering at a detailed carving of a very flexible couple in the act of pleasuring one another. She looked back at him, her eyes full of wicked promise. "A weekend in Manhattan?"

July 2007

Falling in love with Sara turned out to be as simple as falling asleep in her father's garden. She became his gravity, tethering him to her dizzy whirl around the sun. It was July before he came up for air, but it was a glorious drowning.

Jack passed a beer across the back of badly aging leather sofa, and grabbed the freshly delivered pizza. He dropped down next to Seth, set the pizza on the coffee table, and upped the TV volume to hear Jerry Remy's commentary.

"Should I book you now for the next home series?"

Seth reached for a slice without comment. "They look decent this year."

"I get it. She's hot. And good-crazy."

Seth grinned. "She likes you, too."

"And that photographer you snagged, the lady with the creepy doll pictures? Anything yet?"

"Got her into a community show in Somerville. I'm looking to get her into a couple of places in Western Mass. Sara and I are going out there next weekend to check out some locations."

"Weren't you two in Newport last weekend?"

Seth laughed. "Nope, two weeks back. Last weekend, we drove out to Warden's Bluff."

Jack took a long pull from his beer, and belched softly. "Jesus, you brought her home?"

"My parents spoiled her rotten. Mom even made beignets."

"Your mom cooked? Does Sara get what a big deal that is?"

"She used the mix I sent her from New Orleans." Seth chuckled. "I prepped Sara pretty well. Told her what it was like to grow up in an artist's colony with a hippie painter for a mother."

"Shit." Jack muttered at the television as the Blue Jays put a second runner on base before he looked over at Seth. "So, where to next?"

"Maybe Charleston or Savannah. She just read *Midnight in the Garden of Good and Evil.*"

Seth shrugged. "And she's already thinking about where to go for her semester break at New Years."

"She's really into travel, huh?" Jack tapped the remote against his leg.

Seth caught the deeper inquiry in Jack's question.

"She's spontaneous."

"And loaded."

Seth also caught the note of caution. "It's true. She is. She can afford to go places, and she wants to go. If she wants to bring me along, I'd be an idiot to turn her down."

Jack whooped as the Sox tagged the runners at first and third. "Can't argue with that."

They watched a few innings in a companionable silence, punctuated only with game commentary and spirited smack talk about the Toronto pitcher's mother.

"Want any more?" Jack lifted the pizza box from the glass-top table. A steam blot ghosted away, along with the smell of congealed pepperoni and cheese.

Seth eyed the cooling grease pools. "I'm good."

While Jack was stuffing the pizza box into his fridge, Seth said the thing he'd been needing to say to someone for a couple of weeks. Someone who wasn't Sara.

"I think I'm in love with her."

The inning switched in the commercial break, with Matsuzaka back on the mound.

"Be careful, okay?" Jack handed Seth a fresh bottle of Harpoon. "She's definitely special, but I can't help thinking there's something she's not telling you."

Seth tossed his bottle cap into a wooden bowl on the coffee table, absentmindedly enjoying the buttery grain of burled oak. "It's only been a couple of months. If she's got secrets, she'll tell me when she's ready."

LABOR DAY WEEKEND 2007

"Even kale tastes better in the Pioneer Valley." Sara giggled and scooped up a spoonful of pearled couscous stew. "And eating it means I can have the peach-bourbon *crème brulée* for dessert."

Seth sliced into the stack of beefsteak tomatoes and buffalo mozzarella they were sharing. he could smell the basil leaves and olive oil as he speared a forkful. The end of summer was a glorious time. "Have all the desserts on the menu if you want. We're celebrating."

Sara slurped her stew appreciatively and raised her wineglass in tribute. "Thank you, Peregrine Fowler, for your bizarre, but marketable, talent and your unfortunately punny name."

Seth clinked his own glass to her hers. "To Peri."

Sara sipped. When her gaze returned to his, her expression was soft, but murky. "And to Seth, the love of my life, on his birthday. You are only twenty-five once."

His whole body seized up in joy. He nearly dropped his wine, and he felt his cheeks rise in an inevitable, goofy smile. She loved him. Out loud.

"I love you, Sara."

There were answering tears in her eyes when she smiled over the rim of her glass. "I got you something." She leaned down to paw through the contents of her purse, then righted herself with a pale turquoise Tiffany & Co. box in one hand. "Happy birthday."

He took the box and slid the creamy ribbon from around the lid. Inside, tucked carefully between layers of batting, was a silver keyring with a single Schlage key already looped on it next to the *Please Return to Tiffany & Co.* oval tag.

"A key?"

She reached into her purse and pulled out a sheet of folded paper, sliding it across the table. He unfolded the paper with no idea what to expect. They'd never so much as spoken of living together, though Seth wanted nothing more, except perhaps—in his most honest heart —to marry her.

It was not, however, an apartment lease.

It was a commercial real estate listing sheet for a small, second-story office space on Charles Street. He blinked at the photos of shiny hardwood, white mouldings, and a huge divided-light window that looked out onto Beacon Hill's gas lamps and brick sidewalks.

"Sara?"

"The Weston Portfolio's offices. Ready when you are." She clapped giddy hands. "Yours for five years. Or less, if you need something else. I had my money guy set up some kind of trust. It's not permanently tied to the lease."

The table swam, his body tensed. Gratitude swamped him, along with a punch of anger and fear. He wasn't ready; he didn't deserve such a gift. *How could he ever repay it? How could he ever accept it?*

"Don't tell me you can't." Sara pinned him to the back of his chair with her gaze; there was a weariness there. Older than the world, as the expression went. "You can. And taking it will make me happy. I didn't earn my money, Seth. I have it because my mom died. I'm not going to squander it, but I'm going to do things with it that bring me joy. Things I think my mom would have done." She released him, and focused for a moment on her bowl. When she looked up, her eyes were damp. "Think of Peri. You can help her make a living. And how many others like her? You're good at it. You've got an eye, and a way with people, and a notion of how to market and sell. All you need is capital."

She was right. He could see it as clearly as the photos on the listing sheet. A bouquet of artists, a beautiful space in which to manage their careers, a place to make a name for himself. Maybe even someday a gallery of his own.

"Okay. You're amazing. Crazy, but amazing." He folded the listing sheet and tucked it under the Tiffany box. "Tell me about her. Your mom."

The sadness faded from her eyes.

"She laughed. All the time. And sang. I'm not even sure she realized how often she sang to herself. She made my dad smile when his students were giving him fits. Kip and I were her partners in crime in everything. Birgit worshipped her."

Seth watched Sara's mouth curve in the telling.

"She laughed and sang and danced right up until the cancer took her. She flung joy in the face of death and just lived the hell out of her life." Sara closed her eyes, savoring some private image of her mother's love for a moment. "She taught me everything I will ever need to know about grace, and I miss her all the time."

He reached across the table to take her hand. "We'll build it all together. We'll make your mother proud. I promise." The question came out of his heart before his head had time to slow him down. "Marry me, Sara. We'll dance and sing and laugh for the rest of our lives."

She squeezed his fingers in return, a kind of broken smile quivering on her lips as a hint of the earlier sadness crept back across her face. "I'm not ready to get married yet, but I love you, Seth. Ask me in a year." She took a deep breath. "Ask me in a year."

Seth tried not to let his grief show, but she must have seen it in his expression.

"I love you. I'm not leaving. I just can't be engaged yet. Please trust me?"

"I do." Jack's warning echoed in memory, and Seth tamped it down. "Should we flag down the server and see about that peach-bourbon creme brulée?"

∾

JANUARY 2008

"By the time we stop at Peet's for coffee, it'll be eight," Seth muttered to himself, taking the stairs up to the second floor of Sara's father's house two at a time. "If we get to Quebec City by dinner, it'll be a fucking miracle."

At least four times in the last ten minutes, Sara had forgotten something she had to have.

The car door slammed as he entered the room Sara used as a study. He'd asked her to wait for him, frustrated by her uncharacteristic forgetfulness and fretting.

He was rifling through receipts, pens, hair pins, Werther's caramels, highlighters—the detritus of Sara's academic career all contained in the center desk drawer when she called to him.

"Seth?"

He could imagine her standing indignantly on the kitchen's Mexican tile floor, reflected morning sunlight bouncing off the ruthlessly clean Viking onto the unruly curls that escaped her casually twisted "traveling hair."

Where was her passport? He slammed the drawer shut and hauled open the file drawer to the right.

Her feet pounded up the stairs. "Seth! I said I'd get the damn passport!"

The folder was marked "Personal" which seemed a logical place to find her passport; he flicked it open.

He pulled the image from the folder without thinking.

"Seth," she whispered, a hand on his shoulder. His shoulder which suddenly seemed so far from his hand. Blood rushed behind his eyes; her voice was wobbly and distant.

She took the film from him. "You weren't meant to see that."

He couldn't look at her, couldn't see more than the inverse images in stark grayscale. The medical coding, the neurology jargon: meaningless. Only the shocking white mass grasping among the gray wrinkles, and her name in boldface.

Cabot Sara Evans

"Seth." Her voice came into sharp, cruel focus. "We have a seven hour drive to talk about this."

He was incapable of motion, until she bent suddenly, slipped the image into her desk drawer, and slammed it, startling him. She brandished her passport in her right hand.

"You promised me a night at the ice hotel for my birthday." She tugged at the ends of her scarf, pulled a wayward curl away from her lip, and walked out of her study. Her voice floated back to him.

"And as I might not have another one, we should get going."

Seth hauled the car onto the snowy shoulder somewhere in Quebec, after four and a half hours of stunted conversation and his own awkward misery. He shoved the gearshift into park, ignoring the shudder as the tires met icy asphalt. He turned to face Sara, who met his gaze with unflinching eyes.

"Jack warned me you were hiding something." He slammed the

steering wheel. "I gave you the benefit of the doubt. I asked you to *marry* me..."

His voice broke as the words ran out, and Sara waited while he cried. He didn't notice she'd turned off the music until he was quiet himself. She was still watching him with a peaceful kind of melancholy.

"When people know you're dying, you're already dead."

Seth started to contradict her, but she cut him off.

"It's true. I've been dead all morning. You're already thinking about life after me, even if those thoughts are grief and sadness and longing. Even the anger you're choking on, it's anger because I am going to be dead. I'm already dead, and no matter how hard you try, I'll never really be alive to you again." She cupped his cheek in her palm. "I was dying that night at the Phoenix. You walked over, and I was alive again. I wanted to be alive."

Seth pushed her hand away. "You let me fall in love with you."

"I let us fall in love with each other." She wound her hands into the tails of her plaid scarf. "Maybe it was selfish, and yes. I lied by omission." She spoke without looking at him, gazing out the windshield at the flurries swirling around passing cars. "What would you have said if I'd just come out with it: 'You can't call me in three days, because I might be dead?'"

"You didn't give me a choice in the matter."

"No, I didn't." She turned back at him, flushed, her eyes glittering. Her voice crescendoed. "I saw something in your face that made me want to be happy—stupidly happy—for a night, a week, six months, a year. However long I had, and I took the chance."

She sucked in a chestful of air, and the fight was gone from her. "You'll miss me for a while, Seth. I can only speculate as to whether there will be something of me to miss anyone once I leave you."

He couldn't stop the venom. "And the office? The trust? Am I your dying charity project, Sara?"

She reeled back, tears spilling down her cheeks. "I don't care if you give it all away. The money and the office were a gift. Because I believe in you and I can help you. I can't fucking take it with me, but if you don't want it, by all means. Give it away."

Her acceptance of his anguish deflated him, and she was right. He couldn't look at her without wondering about the void she would leave in his life.

"Your father, Kip, Birgit? They're just going to let you do this?"

She took his hand across the center console. "I told you, Seth. I learned everything I know about grace from my mom, even grace in finite moments. They know, too. We all watched this kill her, too."

"I'm sorry." His voice broke again, and he reached for her. "I'm so sorry."

She leaned into his arms, leaned into his kiss. He tasted mingled tears on their lips.

"Thank you," she whispered against his mouth.

He touched his forehead to hers. "For what?"

"For kissing me like I'm alive."

Seth cradled her face in his hands. "I love you."

Sara's stomach rumbled, and weak laughter bubbled between them. "I love you, too. I'll love you more when you feed me something extravagant and French in Old Quebec City."

MARCH 2008

Seth slipped out to the loading dock for a breath of fresh air. The gallery's climate control kept the art safely cocooned, but it couldn't filter out the inane babble of the crowd at Peregrine's opening.

The air was bitter, sharp with cold, too cold even for snow, though the clouds, steel gray, like the warehouse door, hung low. February's frozen onslaught bled relentlessly into March, and Seth was beginning to think winter would never let him go.

He wasn't sure he cared. The weather suited his grief.

Peregrine would be looking for him. Regardless of his own suffocating emotions, he needed to get back to her. Peri was fragile and unpredictable, but she was also deeply empathetic, and might very well walk out of her own show to check up on him.

He put his hand on the door handle, the chill driving straight through his flesh. It wasn't Peri he thought of when the cold burned his skin. It was another woman, another door handle.

Sara, warm and pulsing with humor and desire, wearing nothing but his pinstriped dress shirt, pressed against the antique five-panel door to her bedroom. He'd reached for the cold glass knob with one fumbling hand, the other attempting to part the buttons. She'd have known putting it on after her shower would drive him crazy.

"I'll never be able to wear this shirt again," he'd whispered against her mouth between kisses.

She'd pushed him away, reached for his belt buckle, looked up at him through her lashes.

"I want you to wear it. I want to think of you, attempting to be professional, wearing this shirt, remembering slipping it off my shoulders, smelling my perfume."

Impatiently biting her lower lip, she'd tugged at the button of his rumpled chinos.

"Sara." He was a beggar.

He'd threaded his hand into the hair at her nape and brought their mouths together. The glass knob had turned in his hand, and they'd stumbled backwards into her bedroom.

Under his hand, nearly frostbitten in his reverie, the handle turned, the hinges protesting. Peri's clear eyes, too heavily lined, peeked around the door.

"Seth? Are you okay?"

He snapped back into the cold reality of late winter in Boston. The warehouse stoop in SoWa had never felt so far from Sara's Brattle Street house.

"I just came out for some air."

"Seth, honey. It's too cold, and you shouldn't be alone." Peri's throaty, delicate doll-voice reprimanded him. She pushed the door open to usher him inside.

Jack was waiting for him on the gallery floor. He was flying unexpectedly solo, and wearing his serious expression.

"Hey."

Jack pocketed his hands and looked around at Peri's work on the walls. "Interesting. Creepy as hell, but interesting. Do you think you can sell her in New York?"

Seth felt something like curiosity kindle in the hollow of his chest. "What do you mean?"

"Kearney-Mulligan has offered me a position in the Midtown office. I signed a lease on a loft, but I could use a roommate." He put a hand on Seth's shoulder. "And you could use a break from this town."

Seth tried to ignore the pinch in his gut at the idea of leaving Boston. "Congrats, man. I know you were hoping for that offer."

Peri drifted back to him with a wiry, bespectacled man on her arm. "Excuse me, Seth, honey."

Jack smiled indulgently and squeezed Seth's arm. "We'll talk."

❧

June 2008

The freight elevator creaked closed and clanked its way down again as Seth set down the last box from his former apartment, his gaze drawn to a fanciful three-legged milking stool. Like something from a fairytale with its twists and bends, the glowing wood grain appeared to have grown up out of an enchanted forest floor. It reminded him of the bowl Jack always kept on his coffee table for bottle caps.

He'd have to ask Jack who the artist was. And if he had representation.

Jack's Manhattan loft rental was probably too much for the two of them, even with Jack's generous salary. Jack was already talking about finding a third guy to share.

Seth sat down inside the partitioned area that was his bedroom, and opened the box he'd carried up. He immediately wished he hadn't.

Sara had popped into the bathroom, peeling back the shower curtain to say goodbye while he was rinsing shaving cream from his face.

He'd touched the tip of her nose. "You're pale. You feeling okay?"

She'd wrinkled her face up at his wet hand dripping on her sweater, but her smile came easily. "Fine. I'll see you tomorrow?"

"You want me to pick you up?"

She'd appraised his nakedness, and grinned. "Right now I'd rather skip Jack's girlfriend's band's show and do wicked things to that body."

He'd leaned out to kiss her—a long, hot tangle of tongue and lips and steam—and they parted breathlessly. "We'll do both."

"I love you, artboy."

"Love you, too." He shivered at the chill in the bathroom air, despite the steam and Sara's kiss. "Sara? Don't forget your scarf. It's nasty out there," he called as she dropped the shower curtain and closed the bathroom door behind her.

The scarf still hung over the arm of the sofa when he left for work.

Birgit had met him at the door to Sara's father's house the following day, her red ringed eyes telling him there would be no concert.

Seth couldn't stop his hand caressing the plaid merino of Sara's forgotten Burberry scarf, haphazardly tossed in among her abandoned copy of *Doctor Zhivago*, marked with a dog-eared postcard of Van Gogh's *Café Terrace at Night*.

The freight elevator ground to a halt again, signaling Jack's return. Seth pressed the box flaps together, slid it under a nearby chair, and whispered hello to Sara's ghost, set adrift into his new life on the scent of *Coco*.

~

From the World of Thornton Vermont

A GILDED PROMISE

Cameron D. Garriepy

NEWPORT, RHODE ISLAND

AFTER THE EVENTS OF DAMSELFLY INN

Fifty years, Elisha McNair whispered to her champagne flute. Fifty years, and they were still in love.

Her grandparents spun gently around the ballroom to the tune of an elegant Austrian waltz. The whole evening had a Merchant-Ivory film feel. The gilded ballroom at Rosecliff was dotted with three dozen intimate tables for six, each one draped in silver and cream, anchored by exclamations of blushing roses in tall, slim vases to allow conversation and champagne toasts to flow freely.

A White Tie Celebration of Love, the invitation requested, and her grandparents' friends and family had risen to the occasion. The room fairly shone with it. It began with the couple on the dance floor and drifted over the crowd like magic. The glowing confection of tables and food and music was nearly overshadowed by the glitter of jewels and shimmer of silks, but nothing overshadowed her grandparents' love.

Elisha indulged in a heartbeat of profound loneliness. Even here, amongst her beloved family, wrapped in an embarrassment of wealth, such devotion eluded her.

"Elisha?"

The hand at her elbow brought her out of her thoughts with a start and her wine sparkled right over the rim of the flute. She followed the hand back to the tuxedoed man to her left.

"Your grandmother was the first woman I proposed to." His wry smile wrinkled the corners of his eyes and dimpled his right cheek. "I was devastated when she told me she was far too old to break in a new puppy."

Elisha tilted her head, squinting. There was something familiar about him, but she couldn't place the man.

"She offered me a *petit four* from the sideboard, and told me to go find her granddaughter. Your nanny had already taken you back to your parent's cottage, so I had to amuse myself. I didn't find you–"

The memory came suddenly, vividly to mind. "The cocktail party for Daddy's college roommate!" She'd been seven, tired from tennis and sailing, and had been sent to bed before the guests of honor had arrived. "You found me the next day, at the pool. You cannonballed and soaked my lunch!" She laughed. He'd come up sputtering, already laughing, and she'd jumped in right on top of him for splashing her dolls and their luncheon.

He grinned. "You do remember."

A golden summer, more than twenty years before, spent at her grandparents' compound in Jamestown. Mimi had opened a chest of antique dolls, complete with clothes and an exquisite little tea set. Elisha had had lunch with the dolls every day for a month, until Benjamin had come to stay.

"Congratulations on the book," he said, raising his glass to her. "When the *Times* reviewed it, I told everyone I knew that I'd been friends with you for half a summer when we were kids, that you were a notably better tennis player at seven than I am now, but that I could always find trouble faster."

And he had. He'd led her on every mad adventure she'd never dared before his arrival. They'd ventured into the root cellars of the old barns, raced each other through the salty Narragansett Bay air on borrowed bicycles, dared one another to hike farther, swim faster, turn up dirtier for dinner... He'd jumbled up the framework of her very structured days and let her taste a little wildness. He'd been something like a brother, something like an innocent crush. He'd been hers. Until his parents had left, and he'd never come back.

She laid a hand on his arm.

"I know it was a long time ago, but I was so sad when I heard what had happened to your parents." She sipped her champagne to hide the hitch in her voice. "No one told me until the next summer when I asked when you were coming to stay."

Benjamin's expression clouded, but he smiled. "Thank you. My Mom's sister never really liked the *richies*—her words, not mine. So she kind of cut me off from Dad's friends after I went to live with her."

The waltz had given over to a Fifties sock hop number. Mimi and Grandpère were still on the floor, and a number of other couples had joined them, showing off moves people just didn't learn anymore. Elisha set her empty flute on the silver tray offered by one of the waitstaff, before turning back to him.

"I'm glad you're here. How did they find you, after all of these years?"

"I thought they might have told you. I got my island back." He took a fresh glass from the same tray. "I bought the property adjacent to theirs last year. I'm having the house restored."

She smiled at the memory of her childhood friend laying claim to the place that shared his last name: *My island. Jamestown.* She wasn't the only one enjoying professional success, then. He didn't have to be specific. She knew which house he'd bought. The shingle-style home had been falling to ruin for decades, perched on a small spit of land just north of her parents' cottage on the compound. There wasn't nearly the acreage that her grandparents owned, but the place had a faded charm she'd never been able to resist.

It had been empty even that long-ago summer, and they'd explored the abandoned house together, braving rotted floors and broken windows to ghost-hunt in the third floor gables. Elisha had loved the peaked rooflines, and the broad porch that wrapped around the entire first floor. She'd dared him stand with her on the deck that jutted out from the master bedroom on the second floor. They'd both shrieked when the old doors slammed shut behind them, an errant seabreeze substituting for the ghosts they never found.

Benjamin stopped a passing server and waited while she plucked a puff-pastry shell from the tray. The dilled salmon and *crème fraîche* inside melted into the pastry, and she wished she could lick her fingers. As if he'd read her thoughts, Benjamin offered her a cocktail napkin. "When I started inquiring about it, I half expected to find you'd bought it and filled it up with great- grandkids for Marianne and Laurent."

She knew when she smiled up at him that there was a wistful twist in her smile. "I love that house, but my life has never been in Jamestown."

"You're life is in Vermont now, if your grandparents and your book jacket can be believed."

"Book jackets never lie," she laughed. "I am, for the next little while, teaching at Thornton College and working on a second book."

He gave her a pointed look. "I've never been to Vermont."

She hid behind her champagne. Nostalgia and loneliness were dangerous any time. In the ballroom at Rosecliff, awash in love songs and sparkling wine, they were lethal. "I can recommend a great B&B."

"I may take you up on that." He took her glass from her and set it with his on a nearby table, then took her empty hand in his. "For the moment, dance with me, Lee."

The pet name brought a blush; no one called her that.

The boy, whose boldness had changed her life in more ways than he'd ever know, was a man now, and his closeness wasn't lost on her as he led her into the current of dancers. The quiet, sheltered girl who'd come to the Marchand compound on Jamestown to spend a summer with her grandparents while her parents were in the Middle East on business had come away with a new spark of confidence. She'd kindled that confidence as surely as she'd honed her mind and her body.

Benjamin James was flint and steel, then as now.

He held her lightly, easily. She wondered when he'd learned to dance. His casual explanation of his aunt's attitude didn't seem to line up with the formal dance steps. Her own lessons had been conducted in a private ballroom with a dance master who'd taught the same steps since 1955. When Ben twirled her, they laughed together; Elisha surrendered to the moment and let the lights and crystal blur around them.

The music wound down and Ben led her toward fresh champagne. "Tell me you're staying with your grandparents this weekend." Their fingers brushed, lingered on the stem as he handed her a glass. "I want to see you again."

Disappointment flavored the sip she took to delay the inevitable. Her life, as she'd said, was not here. No matter how handsome the man, how sweet the memories, how beloved the house he now called his own. "I'm not. I'm driving back first thing in the morning. I have to teach a class in the afternoon."

"I knew he'd find you," Marianne Marchand slipped an arm through her granddaughter's as her husband of half a century reached out to shake Benjamin's hand.

"The boy's resourceful," Laurent Marchand's voice was still touched with his native accent. He bent to kiss Elisha's cheek. "*Bonjour, ma p'tite.*"

Elisha leaned into her grandfather's embrace. "*Bonjour, Grandpère.*"

She then watched as her grandfather and her first crush launched into a neighbourly discussion of property lines and local ordinances while she and her grandmother looked on. Elisha tried to follow their rapid fire conversation, but she noticed her grandmother had given up and was watching her husband with an exasperated fondness that Elisha thought might have been the secret to fifty years of marital satisfaction.

"Elisha, you will come back this summer for a visit, won't you?" Her grandmother glanced pointedly at Ben, "Or at the very least invite Benjamin to Vermont? You two were so close that summer."

"I don't know, Mimi." She sipped at the champagne again, but it barely ghosted her lips. She needed air. "Excuse me a moment?"

Her grandmother patted her arm, and began the process of extracting her husband from his tirade about the municipal council. Elisha slipped into the crowd, making her way out to the foyer.

She passed Rosecliff's famous heart-shaped grand stairs and exited through the main door. The grounds were cool and dim; the water feature sang its burbling tune. It was nearly midnight, and Bellevue Avenue was quiet. The party's glow beckoned, but the room had lost its luster for her. Benjamin's presence had woken too many emotions.

She drifted away from the house, drawn to the peace of the fountain. Peace interrupted by gentle footsteps on the peastone, his voice on the sea air.

"I thought I'd lost you again." He'd been a determined boy, too. "Ben..."

He crossed through the blue shadows, the fallen dew shining on his shoes, to pull her into his arms. The kiss was everything she'd been longing for an hour before. She was drowning in everything she couldn't have. Not now, and she was far too realistic to think he'd still be waiting for her in their house when–if–she was ready to let him set her soul on fire.

"Ben–"

He stopped her. "It's a lot, but we'll get used to it." His smile gleamed in the darkness.

"What?"

"Love at second sight." His voice was light, but she heard no mockery there. "I didn't expect it, either, but I trust it."

She wanted to scream. "I'm leaving for Vermont in the morning. I have a life there, and you've just bought a house that desperately needs you."

He kissed her again, gently, on her lips, at her temple. "The house needs my bank account. It wants you." His lips brushed hers again, feather-light and searing."I want you."

"I'm leaving–" She felt like a broken record.

"For Vermont. In the morning." He finished her thought. "But I'm not giving up that easily. Not now. Not with what I'm feeling tonight. I promise. I'll visit. Soon." Ben squeezed her fingers. "And I'm going to prove this to you."

...not the end just yet.

STAR OF WONDER

STAR OF WONDER

AFTER THE EVENTS OF SWEET PEASE

vy Brennan's foot sank through the powdery crust, and a fresh, slushy wetness seeped into her fleece socks. She sighed deeply and hollered into the darkness beyond the beam from her club-sized Maglite. When nothing but her own weary shouting echoed back to her through the woods, she groaned skyward.

The Pleiades were unsympathetic, but Ivy giggled, imagining the seven starry sisters chasing four nanny goats through the heavens.

If only it *were* funny. Her girls would be in trouble if she didn't find them soon. She recalled from her books that the falling snow was more stressful on her still-young herd than cold alone.

"Nyx! Io! Ceres! Iphi!"

She paused, stilling her breathing and leaning into the quiet, hoping to hear a frantic bleat, or even the wretched screaming that signaled their displeasure. A crescent moon peeked from between the bare branches of a scraggly maple tree, but it offered her nothing useful in the way of light.

She chafed her gloved hands together, balancing the flashlight under her chin and wishing she'd double checked the barn door before the storm. Tony was many things, but not always good with latches.

"Nyx? Iphi?" She called. If she could just figure out which way they'd gone, she was sure they would hear her and be clever enough to follow her voice to warmth and safety. "Io? Ceres?"

This time, a faint goaty noise caught her ear.

She held still again, waiting for another sound to guide her, at the same time scolding herself for going so far into the frosty woods that she could no longer see the glow of the barn lights.

Ivy was gearing up to call the goats again when another flashlight beam cut across her own. Its bearer was tall and broad-shouldered, but without direct light, it was hard to make out much more. A shadowy, blunt object rose slightly from one shoulder, as if strapped across his back.

Her mind went involuntarily to the heroes in her mother's novels: tall, broad, and bearing enormous broadswords. When your mother was a New York Times Bestselling, RITA-awarded, internationally-translated author of historical Scottish romance, it was hard not to imagine burly Highland warriors as a default. She wondered hysterically if a stern Highlander would be useful in a dark Vermont forest on a cold night, when your beloved goats had gone on walkabout in December's first real storm.

"Hello?" Not a Highlander then. His accent was soft, his voice deep without being gruff, but he was definitely a local. "Are you looking for these ladies?"

He stepped into the beam of her light, revealing a clean-shaven face between a thick knit scarf and a black watch cap, a performance-fabric anorak, and jeans over Sorel packs. The object on his back was a thick black cylinder. A thin rope was looped around the necks of her four errant goats, like one of the shared rope leashes Ivy associated with pre-schoolers.

Ceres bleated. All four of them danced a bit on their hooves.

Ivy reached for the stranger's improvised lead. "I am. I don't know how you found them, but thank you."

"The bandit—" Here the stranger waved an impatient hand at the goat in the front of the line, "nearly knocked me into Fuller Creek while I was looking at Jupiter and Regulus."

He spun on his heel, and marched off into the darkness, leaving her holding the rope. Nyx meh'd softly, peering after her rescuer from her black-masked eyes.

A strawberry blonde in a pencil skirt and crisp white blouse was at the stove when Ivy returned.

Ivy took note of her baby sister's seamed stockings and the stiletto heels sitting on one of her kitchen chairs. She stomped the snow from her boot treads and shrugged out of her down jacket.

Phlox was stirring a steaming pot and humming to herself. She looked over at Ivy, who was bent over to pull off her wet socks. "Cocoa?"

"When did you get in?"

Phlox sipped from her stirring spoon, then tipped the contents of the pot into two lumpy stoneware mugs. "Twenty minutes ago or so. You didn't see my car?"

Ivy took the mug from her sister, her fingers tracing her own name, carved childishly into the pottery before it had been glazed, nearly thirty years before. The one in Phlox's manicured hands read *Jack*. Not for the first time, Ivy wished her uncle had lived long enough to know Phlox as well as he had her.

"I came in from the barn. The goats got out and wandered off. I didn't realize it until after the snow started."

"Ivy, you didn't have to get livestock…"

Ivy sat down at the kitchen table. The cocoa was thick, perfectly chocolaty, and blissfully warm. "I want them. I'm serious about this."

Phlox rinsed the pot out in the deep farmer's sink before blowing the steam curls from the surface of her cocoa. "I brought your box of ornaments from Mom's, are you going to have a tree?"

"Tony's going to cut one and bring it over. His family owns a little cut-your-own tree farm up near Vergennes."

"Tony?" Her sister's man-antennae extended almost visibly.

Phlox meant well. Ivy knew that, but she couldn't stop the sigh escaping her lips. "Tony is a semi-retired septuagenarian who lives down the road a few houses. He's helping me out a few days a week.

He also hands out saws and makes change for his daughter and son-in-law's tree farm during the season."

"I see." Phlox's lips pursed, and her eyelids fluttered in that way that meant she was working out logistics in her head. "I'm going to get my jammies on. How early do your…goats…get up in the morning?"

Ivy laughed. "Early enough."

"It's only ten. We'll put in a movie and have a sister-snuggle, then I'll get up early with you and learn something about farming as penance for keeping you up." Phlox drained her cocoa and set the mug on the washboard.

Ivy watched her sister's still enviably firm tush wiggle its way down the hall to the stairs and wondered just how helpful Phlox would be in the barn at five a.m.

Sterling West woke to the whining buzz of a chipper and bashed his head against the low eave under which he'd been sleeping.

He rubbed his head and swung his feet over the side of the bed. He'd been dreaming of goats and giants playing jacks. Who the hell let their goats wander around in the forest, never mind when it was snowing?

A woman with color in her cheeks and a halo of curls peeking out of her hat, in this case.

He'd been up near the source of Fuller Creek, in a hilltop clearing scattered with huge boulders, halfway to Jupiter through his telescope, when the bleating had pulled him back to earth. The masked goat had nearly butted him backward into the creek.

Sterling laid back against his pillow and contemplated the goatherd. Hard to tell, but he'd have guessed around his age. Not quite long in the tooth yet, anyway. He might have let forty pass him by, but there was nothing wrong with a little life experience. Especially when it came to matters between a man and a woman.

Julia had lacked for life-experience, and its resulting wisdom, but he'd learned that too late.

That lesson was why he was home for the winter, helping out with his cousin's tree farm and sleeping in his uncle's attic bedroom. His own lack of wisdom had left him homeless at Halloween, with nothing but his clothes, his laptop, and his telescope. Couch surfing only lasted so long before you had to go where they don't turn you away.

He wondered if the woman and her goat-goddesses were well-known. He'd been unpleasant to her, which had more to do with not getting the shot he'd wanted than her or her wandering pets.

"Junior? You up yet?" Uncle Tony's holler was undiminished by his advancing years.

He stood, then thought better of it. The scrubbed pine floors were frigid. "Yeah, Uncle T. I'm up."

"Good. Get your ass down here, we've got trees to sell."

When he got down to the kitchen, there was fresh coffee steaming in an uncapped travel mug. His uncle was pulling two apple fritters from the toaster oven.

Tony dropped the pastries in a brown paper sack and waved at the fridge. "There's milk in there if you want. Then we have to go. I told Miss Ivy I'd bring her a tree."

Sterling felt the corners of his mouth twitch. Tony had mentioned his neighbor, Miss Ivy, no less than fourteen times in forty-eight hours. Just went to show, crushes didn't belong exclusively to the very young. He wondered what sort of lady Tony's Miss Ivy was. Blue hair with a salon-tight permanent wave? Gray-braided hippie in flannels and Bean boots? Proper matron, aging sprite?

It would be a treat to find out about his uncle's ladylove. Nothing cured a broken heart better.

A ride-along with Tony was like strapping into a tourist attraction. Sterling sat back, watching the changes in his hometown roll by while Tony talked.

As they passed a newly constructed commercial property with a coffee shop, a Chinese take-out counter, and a Rite-Aid: "Golden Prawn's still the best for takeout, but there's that new little place that's got Vietnamese food..." As they passed a winery that had been a dairy farm in his youth: "That bakery from Thornton moved in there last year. Fancy, but Alice likes the *croissants*." Sterling allowed himself a little smile at his uncle's drawn-out over-pronunciation of the French.

Tony turned down the dirt track to Jack Hennessey's old place, and Sterling sat up. "Your Miss Ivy bought Jack's place?"

"That's right, forgot to mention that. Mind's not the steel trap is once was." Tony punched him genially in the shoulder. "Ivy's family to Jack through his sister, the one who writes those paperbacks with the half-naked Scotsmen on the covers."

Sterling adjusted his mental image of Miss Ivy to account for Jack's romance-writer sister. Bookish, maybe, with scarves and drapey sweaters.

The hard-packed driveway in front of Jack Hennessey's homestead was empty. He and Tony unloaded a six-foot blue spruce from the back of the pick up and Tony headed around back to the shed, where he was certain he would find the stand Miss Ivy had picked up down at the garden store.

Sterling noted the freshly shored up barn and the new coat of white paint on the house. Miss Ivy was brightening up the old bachelor pad, anyway. The meh-ing of the goats mingled with the clucking chatter of chickens pecking at the cold ground near the coop adjacent to the barn. He did a quick mental hike through Jack's woods towards the Stone Garden and Fuller Creek. Those goats had wandered a full mile from home in the snow.

Did goats stargaze? The fanciful question surprised him. He'd learned to bite back his whimsy. Julia hadn't appreciated it.

Tony came back with the stand and a key. "Lets shake it out here, then set it up near the window in the living room. Ivy'll like the surprise."

Inside, Sterling recognized the ancient appliances and bare bones furniture that Jack had kept around the place, but there were touches of modern femininity: a high-end coffee maker plugged in on a new countertop next to the stove, a woodcut print by a local artist on one wall, cozy blankets and pillows on the stark chairs, and an IKEA rocking chair with a foot rest near the fireplace. Flowers in a pewter pitcher on the table.

It was the shoes that surprised him most. Miss Ivy was fashionable. Julia would have coveted the nude patent leather pumps that were left on the kitchen chair.

"Junior, you gonna stare at those shoes all morning or put some water on for this tree?" Tony already had the tree in the stand by the window and was making sight-line adjustments. Sterling grabbed the kettle from the stove and filled it up, feeling oddly nostalgic. He'd spent a fair amount of time making tea for Jack when his late mentor was stubbornly clinging to his last days in his quiet home. He missed the man, more than he'd thought about in a long time.

Maybe he'd come back by another time and talk to Miss Ivy. It would be nice to reminisce about Jack with someone who'd been his family.

Four straight days of Phlox's company reminded Ivy why she'd left the counseling practice she'd worked so hard to build. Her sister spent her days surfing the arteries of modern life as a social media manager for a popular U.S. Senator. Ivy knew Phlox worked incredibly hard, but she also knew her sister thrived in the fast, ever-shifting world of internet branding and message marketing; she used Uber and knew where to eat and who to wear. For Ivy, though, the noise of the city had left her breathless and weary at the end of every day, exhausted from battling the demons wrought in others by the hectic, frantic lives they all lived.

"You look awful," Phlox pointed out from where she was perched on the Poang rocker by the fire, poring over the Senator's Twitter feed.

Ivy laughed out loud. She knew she stank, she'd been mucking the coop and pulling the last of the winter garden. She had sweet, nearly scarlet carrots still coming up in her cold-framed vegetable patch; her pride in them was mildly embarrassing. Far more so were her chicken manure-stained pants.

She gathered her breath in what she hoped wasn't a wheeze. Thirty-seven wasn't that old. "Thanks, sister."

Phlox looked up, suddenly aware of her own words. "Aw, Iveeeeeee…" She sprang up from her chair and wrapped Ivy in a burrowing hug. "Let's go out. There must be somewhere to go out, right?"

"You know what? There is."

She was sure Phlox hadn't meant hiking by moonlight when she'd said, "…go out," but Ivy knew two things, Jupiter was south-southwest of the gibbous moon in an icy clear sky, and the Stone Garden was the place to see it. She carried snacks and a bottle of wine in her pack, and felt the full weight of a day's labor in her knees and quads. Phlox had a pair of camping pads rolled up and slung cross-body on her back, and was striding through the night forest as if she'd hiked every day of her twenty-six years.

Benevolent hatred was totally a thing, wasn't it?

When they reached the point where the cart road up from the homestead opened into the clearing, they saw that they were not alone in their pursuit of celestial events. Picking his way out from the deer track that climbed up from Snake Mountain Road, was the stranger who'd rescued her goats. She was sure of it.

Her certainty vanished as soon as her sister's voice rang out over the clearing.

"Sterling?" Phlox was staring at the goat-rescuer with her mouth open.

The man stopped short, squinting into what moonlight there was. His gaze moved between Ivy and Phlox, coming to rest on Phlox's R.E.I.-catalogued person with an expression that reminded Ivy of a cornered animal.

"Phlox?"

Phlox's smile lit up her face. "What are you doing here?"

Phlox and the goat-rescuer talked over one another in their

mutual haste to make sense of one another. Snippets were all Ivy caught.

"Julia never mentioned…"

"Haven't seen her since…"

"Family nearby…"

"…my sister, Ivy."

"Ivy?" The man, Sterling, or so Phlox was calling him, was openly staring. Her hand rose instinctively to tame the flyaway curls escaping her hat, but she forced it down.

"Ivy. Brennan. We met in the woods behind my house a few nights ago."

Phlox squeaked. "You what?"

Ivy waved a careless hand. "The night you arrived. When the girls got out. He found them in the woods. I found him."

"I think I found you." His laugh was gentle, and that smooth low voice carried over the cold air. Ivy hated herself for the thousand fantasies that played out in her imagination in the time it took him to draw his next breath. Her mother's literary legacy, deeply rooted in her own tender heart and fertile brain. *I think I found you.* She'd officially been alone in Jack's cabin too long.

Sterling was leaving. "I'm sorry I disturbed your outing. Excuse me."

Phlox stepped forward just as Sterling turned back toward the deer track. "Don't go. Stay. Ivy's nice. So am I, no matter what you think of my friends."

Ivy's nice. Wasn't that the truth. So nice, she was the easiest woman in the world to friendzone, to break up with, to politely reject.

Sterling's brow wrinkled. "I don't…No. Thank you. Goodnight."

Much as he had upon delivering the goats into her care, Sterling vanished back into the dark woods without another word.

And that was that: his name was Sterling, and Phlox somehow connected them. Ivy saw that the moon was beginning to sink into the western horizon, drawing Jupiter's bright presence down with her like a lover. They had missed it's brightest moments, but there might still be some meteor showers if they were lucky.

Phlox unrolled her bedroll, sat down, and patted the spot next to her. "You promised me the moon, and wine. Park it."

Ivy busied herself with the midnight picnic. "How, Phlox? How do you know everyone, everywhere you go?"

Phlox shrugged. "Sterling West. He was pretty seriously involved with Julia. She definitely wanted to marry him. You remember Julia? She hired me for that start up after college? A little older than me, full of great ideas and no follow-through? Folded the company to pull an *Eat Pray Love* in the Andes?"

Ivy wracked her brain, and found that she remembered a tumble of sleepy chestnut curls and an effortless, expensive boho-chic wardrobe.

Phlox continued to flesh out her portrait of Sterling West. "He was a freelance IT consultant... Not sure what he specialized in, but he was constantly bailing Julia out when the network crashed. Which it did all the time because she was baffled by technology. I used to have brunch at their place regularly when I worked for Julia, and I remember there being a pretty impressive telescope in their living room. Guess, whatever else he's doing, he's still into stargazing."

A gentle tapping on the barn door's frame pulled Ivy's attention away from Iphi's hooves. She was least docile of the quartet when it came to pedicures.

"Last stall on the right," she called. Phlox, she imagined, back from her spa trip to Stowe with her college roommate, or Tony dropping by to look at one of the endless projects the homestead required.

"I don't think I ever considered you'd have to trim their hooves." Sterling's hot-cocoa voice announced him before he appeared.

Ivy finished rasping the rough bits from her trimming job without looking at her visitor. She'd gotten better since summer. So had her bruised shins. Iphi was a kicker. "I didn't either, before I bought them. I went to a seminar, and the speaker said something like, 'The seat of your pants was made to fly.' I have taken that advice around the block and back this year." She blushed quietly into Iphi's coat.

Why had she said that? He didn't care about seminars or goat hooves. She stowed her tools on a shelf outside the stall as she latched it behind her. "Can I help you with something?"

Sterling was carrying a wreath of cedar and bittersweet berries, wrapped in cream and gold ribbon and tied with a floppy, extravagant bow. "Help? No. I brought you a wreath."

It was the perfect wreath. Soft and wintry, far from the ostentatious ones her former neighbors had favored. It would look beautiful on the cabin's front door. He stood there holding it carefully like an offering, something beseeching in his expression.

Men with offerings apparently made her stammer. "You shouldn't have."

The corners of his mouth turned down to frame his smile with self-deprecating humor. "I absolutely should. My mother would take a switch to my rear end for the way I behaved to you. Twice. My only excuse is a rough year."

"I think I like your mother." Ivy bit back a laugh. *Who says that?* "Sorry."

His smile was a delight. It changed his entire face. "She's a hot ticket, my mom. She'd like that you said that out loud." Sterling let the wreath loop over one arm and pocketed the other hand. "Where would you like this?"

Ivy blinked, then recalled her own manners and reached for the gift. "I'll hang it up on the front door later. In the meantime, can I make you a cup of cocoa?"

He looked as though he would refuse to stay yet again; his yes surprised her.

Sterling fought the urge to put her kettle on for her. The disconnect between her presence and his own history in the cabin pressed on

him. "I'm not good at keeping things to myself, so I'll just tell you: I knew Jack a long time ago. I spent a lot of time here just after college."

Ivy opened the broom closet she'd made over into a small pantry and pulled out the cocoa powder. When she turned to him, he tried not to notice the sheen of unshed tears in her eyes. "You knew Uncle Jack?"

Sterling leaned back against the kitchen sink. "It's all a circle, I guess, or a helix. Tony hired Jack at the warehouse when Jack was in high school. When I was unemployed, angry, and on the brink of getting unruly, Tony sent me to Jack to help him keep up with the place. He didn't tell me how sick Jack was, just that I needed to get my shit together and do something useful with my time."

He watched as Ivy measured milk, sugar, and cocoa into a saucepan, pinching salt from a little copper dish and sprinkling it over the lightly steaming milk. He got the feeling she was busying her hands while she figured out what to say. Her expression was so like her uncle's.

Ivy stirred while she spoke. "We just missed one another, then. I used to come up here for summers when I was a kid, but I was away at boarding school at the end, and my mom didn't want me to know how bad things were." She swiped at her eyes and gave him a wobbly smile. "He sent me postcards. One a week. There was one that last spring before he died, where he mentioned Tony's nephew Junior. He told me he was teaching Junior to use the telescope, that I'd like him. That's you, isn't it?"

Sterling shook his head. *Junior.* For the first time in a lot of years, the nickname didn't rankle. Tony had been calling him that since birth, or so family lore went. Tony's influence was so pervasive that only his mother held out and used his given name, and he wasn't even named after his father.

Once he'd found and taken that first job in D.C., he'd half-jokingly told people he'd run away from home to dodge a bad nickname. Julia had never known it existed. She hadn't cared about Sterling's Vermont tree-farmer family.

Ivy was pouring the hot chocolate into the two lopsided pottery mugs Jack had prized over any others. Sterling knew the story there; Ivy had made them for him half a lifetime ago. He took Jack's from her outstretched hand. "He told me I was a lot like his niece. I was not in my most insightful and sensitive years, then. I think I forgot that almost as soon as he said it."

Her replying smile touched her eyes, but there was sadness in them even so. He heard the attempt at playful humor fall flat in her delivery. "I am infinitely forgettable."

Sterling's chest tightened while Ivy's words hung between them. She was the farthest thing from forgettable: a cloud of honey-colored curls, a sweet smile, and just a hint, under all her layers of warm work clothes, of curves in all the best places. Even better, from where he stood, she knew something of the night sky, and cared about the people around her.

"Jack didn't think so. I'm sorry I didn't listen to him."

Ivy pulled up the plush blanket Phlox had brought her as a housewarming gift, tucking it under her chin, despite the fire that crackled away in the belly of the cast iron wood stove. Kate Winslet was just about to find out that Rufus Sewell was engaged to that other woman, and the bottle of Prosecco her mother had left with her was freshly opened.

All signs pointed to a cozy and intoxicated evening alone. Her sister was in Burlington, seeing a band with someone she knew somehow from the Senator's office, and the goats were snugged up for the night, as were the chickens and the carrots. There was no one to stop her from going straight from *The Holiday* right into *Love Actually*, not one person to judge if she had too much to drink and cried or decided to put on *A Charlie Brown Christmas* at midnight and dance like Snoopy on Schroeder's piano.

And Sterling had stayed for cocoa. Had invited her to watch the Geminid meteor showers in the Stone Garden the next night.

The shrilling of her phone amongst all her snuggly solitude was particularly offensive. She paused her movie and peered a her phone. With a sigh, she pressed the green circle on the screen.

"Hello, Mum."

"Phlox just told me you're spending time with Julia Saxon's husband?" Her mother was not one for small talk.

Ivy felt the sparkling wine go flat in her stomach. "What?"

"Julia. Saxon. Your sister's former employer? Barry's daughter?"

The smallness of the world tightened around her like a noose as she sorted out the details. Barry Saxon was her mother's first literary agent, now retired. Julia was Phlox's boss who'd run off to find inner peace in South America. Her husband was…Sterling?

"I can't talk now, Mum. I'll call you in the morning."

He'd stayed, drinking cocoa and telling her stories about her uncle. He'd helped her hang the wreath. She'd been on the verge of offering him dinner, when he'd glanced at the setting sun and excused himself. Supper with the family.

"The Geminids," he'd said, pausing at the door. "Tomorrow's the peak, and the forecast is perfect. Not too cold, clear, no wind."

"I know," she'd replied, just a little breathless. "I was going to go."

That smile again, surprising, charming. "Let's hike in together."

"Ivy? Don't you hang up on me." Her mother was speaking. "You're not doing this again, are you? Ivy?"

Ivy poised her thumb over the red circle on the screen. "No, Mum. I'm not, but I've really got to go."

She tipped the Prosecco bottle to her lips briefly, then topped off her glass and started the movie again. There was not enough fizzy wine in the world, but maybe, just maybe, there was enough Jude Law.

The rain was pissing him off. Sterling looked up from a long string of code he was unsnarling for a client and cursed the wet streaks rolling down the window. The forecast had been clear for the day and into the evening. The Geminids… and Ivy… were waiting for him and tonight was the night.

He'd had trouble keeping his mind on the updates he was making, because Ivy insisted on creeping into his thoughts. Everything he'd discovered about her teased at his concentration, from her awkward, unfiltered thoughts to the unruly curls she tried so hard to tame. He couldn't help imagining, like a kid with a crush, what it might be like to kiss her under a hundred shooting stars.

When the kitchen door banged open, he nearly knocked his laptop off the table. He'd been daydreaming, knuckle deep in her hair, testing the sweetness of warm lips and cold air, when Tony shattered his mood.

"What in the hell did you do, Junior?"

Sterling blinked at his uncle, then shook his head. "Nothing?"

"Nothing, my ass." Tony yanked a coffee mug from the cabinet and poured cold coffee from the carafe in the coffee maker, then stuck the mug in the microwave and jabbed the panel. The hum of the microwave underscored Tony's accusations. "I was just over at Miss Ivy's place to see about fixing that dripping faucet in the bathroom, and she'd been crying. She was drifting around that house like a ghost. Wasn't until I found her sister in the barn that I got any kind of explanation."

Tony paused to draw breath; Sterling considered asking an obvious question, but thought better of it.

"You've been..." Tony's whole face wrinkled up in consternation, "...flirting with that girl and you're still married to that awful woman who's gallivanting around Mexico with some foreign type?"

At this, Sterling had to intervene. "What the hell, Tony? No. I mean, yes." He shut the laptop and raked his fingers through his hair. "Yes, I guess I was flirting. Badly. But no, goddamn it. Julia divorced me as quickly as the Commonwealth of Virginia would allow. She had inner peace to find in the rainforest and zen to achieve while surfing. She didn't go to Mexico, and Andre was born in Brooklyn."

Tony's rage fizzled out. "Junior, if you intend to continue flirting with that girl, you'd best exercise some damage control. The shit, to put it delicately, has hit the fan."

Sterling was already stowing his computer. His client could wait;

Ivy shouldn't have to. He'd witnessed too much raw fragility in her to allow delay.

He was ready to start lacing his boots, when Tony reached out a hand.

"Going over there now won't do a damn bit of good." Tony sipped from his now steaming mug of coffee. "That sister of hers was about to take her off somewhere for a girl's night. Told me she was going to convince her sister to come back to D.C."

"Shit." Sterling kicked at the boot he'd yet to get on.

"Indeed." Tony grinned. "But there's an upside. You'll have until tomorrow to plan your apology."

The weather cleared by late afternoon, and a cold front poured in over Lake Champlain, frosting the damp ground. Sterling packed for the Geminids with a heavy heart.

Telescope, warm layers, bedroll pad to sit on, the lens adaptor for his phone; he had a mind to take photos of the meteor showers if the sky cooperated.

A woman he barely knew wouldn't be joining him for a solo hike he'd been planning for months. That was no reason not to go. Tony's reminder was fresh in his mind. He could use the quiet time with Regulus, Pleiades, the moon, and the falling bits of asteroid to craft the perfect explanation, and he would knock on Ivy's door once she and Phlox got back from wherever they'd gone off to.

The drive wound along Fuller Creek headed south towards Thornton. The pullover was hard to spot until you got to know the road. The deer track surprised him every time. It was always there, but somehow it toyed with him, its entrance hiding in shadow or behind a low branch, as though it didn't want to be found.

He peered up through the trees as he walked, waiting to catch the first of the shooting stars. There was almost no light pollution up here anyway, never mind out in the middle of the woods. His excitement was dimmed, though, by Ivy's pain. He didn't know how the bad information had found its way to her, but he wanted to make it right before he lost his chance to get to know her better.

He clambered up a stone step and stepped over the spring that fed Fuller Creek, then followed the footpath to its end, where the Stone Garden spread out on the hilltop. The clearing was frosted under the waning moon, the sky a deep, starry indigo and silver expanse above. He was just setting up the telescope when the showers began in earnest, streaking across the night.

He adjusted the scope, and wished again that Ivy was with him. She would have spent time up here, too, with Jack, charting the stars, watching the motions of the solar system and the infinite potential beyond it. He felt that potential between them, and it stole his breath to think he might not get the chance to explain himself.

She wasn't a fly-off-the-handle type, of that he was certain. If he could only get to her before Phlox worked her magic, he could convince her to…to what?

Stay in Vermont to see if the inexplicable draw he felt was something more?

Because she might actually just leave because some guy she'd just met had possibly behaved like a jackass?

Something didn't add up; he'd just been to upset to notice. A woman who learned to trim goat hooves and crooned over her chickens and winter garden wasn't going to pull up stakes over some man she barely knew.

He laughed aloud at his own foolishness, but his mirth was cut short by the rustling of feet in the brush.

Ivy trudged up the cart road that led from her property up the back of the rise to the Stone Garden. She was glad of her mittens and hat. The Arctic air that settled into the valley on the tail of the rainstorm had left a diamond sheen on everything, but it left a bone-aching kind of cold in its wake.

She'd spent the morning going over every conversation she'd had with Sterling, looking for any kind of evidence that he was a married man, for some sign that she had misinterpreted, but she kept coming up empty. By the time Tony showed up with his plumbing tools, she had worked herself into a frenzy over her mother's phone call.

The first time it had happened, it had been an innocent mistake. She and a colleague had drinks at a hotel bar at a conference. She'd had no way of knowing he was cheating on his wife, no way of knowing he was being followed. Being mistaken for the other woman and having her Gibson tossed in her face by an angry wife had been embarrassing, but ultimately harmless.

Jim she had loved. Hopelessly, devotedly. Jim had concealed his true life from her so thoroughly that she'd given him six years of her life. Six years, dreaming of marriage, while he kept a wife and three kids tucked away out in western Maryland.

When her last boyfriend had, after half a year, told her he regretted divorcing his wife and that they were going to make a go of it again, her mother had handed down a hard truth. *Ivy, you are thirty-five years old, and you've yet to have a relationship with a man who was free to love you back. Maybe you're just not meant to get married.* And by getting married, Ivy knew her mother meant having love.

It was a chilling thing, when the reigning queen of historical happily-ever-after told you to quit looking for yours.

She paused to look up at the cascading meteors. She knew what they were. Jack had been clear about the science, but no less reverent for it. *Not shooting stars, Ivy, falling rocks, leaving a burning trajectory as they streak through our atmosphere.* He'd loved them for their fleeting brilliance, for their gorgeous impermanence. They were beautiful, fascinating, humbling, and she would have missed them if she'd been in the city.

She'd left the noise, the hustle, the failed relationships, and set herself up on her own terms. The little farm, Jack's legacy, her cheese-making ambitions, Tony and the other friends she'd found, they meant something to her.

She didn't need to get to know Sterling, but damned if she hadn't wanted to.

Tony had fixed the leaky sink, telling her stories while he worked. She'd gritted her teeth through the endless tale of Sterling's current client, and how disappointed Sterling was to miss the shooting stars because of work.

Had she been on the fence about it, Ceres and Io had led a charge out of the barn when she'd gone to make sure they were safely settled for the night. Sterling would not be abroad in the forest tonight to rescue stray goats; wrangling them on her own firmed her resolve.

He might have to miss the Geminids, but she didn't intend to.

She pushed past a fallen tree branch, shoving it aside with her foot, and stepped out into the Stone Garden to find that she was not alone.

Sterling was kneeling on a camp pad, his telescope forgotten, laughing at her as she emerged from the woods.

"What are you *doing* here?" She hated herself for the whining.

"We've been had, Ivy." Mirth was still splashed across Sterling's face in the moonlight.

Ivy watched the Geminids' burning trajectory behind him. "You're not married, then?"

His laughter softened. "No. Divorced. Lost my apartment because my ex wanted to sell the place. Ended up sleeping in Tony's attic because home is where they have to take you in."

Ivy didn't understand how he could be so amused. "What's funny about that?"

Sterling stood and took a step in her direction, then paused, as if waiting to see her reaction, "Ivy, what did you hear?"

"My mother, she knows your wife—your ex-wife's—father. He was her agent. She heard something from Phlox about you being here, and then she wanted to make sure I wasn't…making a mistake I've made before." Ivy pushed her mittened hands into the pockets of her parka. "Tony told me about how you had a client, and wouldn't be up here. I didn't want to see you if…"

"If I was lying to you by omission? I get that." He tilted his head back as four meteorites streaked overhead. "It's a good one."

Ivy felt a smile tease her cheek muscles. "I didn't want to miss them. They were Jack's favorites."

"Yeah. Me neither." Sterling rolled up on the balls of his feet. "Tony told me you and Phlox were doing some sister overnight trip because you were pissed at me—that Phlox was going to convince you to go back to D.C., and it took me until I was out here on Jack's hill, under his sky, to see that Tony was doing his best to get us both up here tonight in spite of what you heard." He looked down at his toes, then back up at the sky. "I was stupid enough to believe him, that you would actually be talked away from here because I didn't live up to my name."

He was still being funny. And his smile was better in the starlight. "Sterling…"

"Come look," he said, gesturing to the telescope. "Take some pictures if you like."

She passed him, fighting the urge to touch his arm as she did, and knelt by the telescope to adjust the focus. She felt him crouch down beside her while her body curved over the telescope. The falling Geminids filled her field of vision, and she remembered being up here as a child with her uncle.

A burning trajectory, fleeting and brilliant.

She leaned back from the telescope, her arm brushing Sterling's; he'd dropped to his knees on the camp pad. Though he watched the sky, she felt his attention on her when he spoke.

"I'm glad I found your goats by the creek."

Ivy laughed. "I think they found you."

They watched in the sky in silence for a few moments before Sterling replied. "Ivy?"

She turned to him with her heart in her throat, waiting to hear what he would say.

"The Ursids are peaking next week, and I'm tied up with family stuff, but they'll still be visible on Christmas Day. Would you like to join me if the weather's good?

Ivy let go a breath she hadn't been aware of holding, and reached for his hand. Her sister was leaving on Christmas morning to visit their mother. Ivy was looking forward to her quiet again.

"That sounds wonderful."

From the World of Thornton Vermont
SWEET BASIL
CAMERON D. GARRIEPY

THORNTON

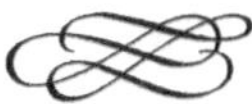

AFTER THE EVENTS OF FAMILY PRACTICE

"Andy, I literally couldn't have done this without you."

Her hair smelled like vanilla and lemon when she kissed his cheek. Five years, he'd worked for Kate Pease at her two locations —first in her downtown pastry shop, then as a manager at her café at Cooper Vineyard—and every day of those five years he'd slept with that distinctive scent in his dreams.

Kate's husband (because of course if you're going to nurture an unrequited passion for your boss, she should be blissfully married) was launching his latest novel at Kate's vineyard café in—Andy checked his smartwatch—fourteen minutes, and so far he'd kept a handle on every detail.

"No problem, Kate. We're all really happy for Ewan."

Kate swept away, the swishy folds of her skirt brushing up against the long legs he'd admired since he was a college freshman.

"She's too old for you."

He hadn't seen Danny--*Danielle*, he mentally corrected himself. Someday he'd remember that she was going by Danielle now--in weeks, not since she'd gone back to school after spring break, but there she was beside him, a tray of bud vases for the buffet tables perched on her shoulder. She was right, but that didn't mean he didn't fall in love with Kate again on a daily basis.

"Shut up, Danny."

"Whatever." She shrugged and continued past him.

She'd cut her hair—short—and dyed it platinum blonde since her last shift. He'd liked it long and dark, especially the secret shocks of violet you only saw when she put it up, but this suited her, too.

"Andy?" Margot, who ran the downtown location, peeked out from the kitchen. "Can I borrow a couple of staffers? I need to bring the cake in from the van."

"Sure thing, Margs."

And just like that, it was showtime. Kate was counting on him.

Events meant keeping his head in the game, but two hours in without a hitch meant he could step back and breathe. He paused by the bar to survey the room, his eyes lingering on Kate, who swayed with her husband on the rented dance floor.

Danny wove through the tables collecting empty glasses, stopping to deposit her tray on a folding stand nearby. She elbowed him playfully, following the direction of his gaze. "If we weren't such good friends, I'd say something about how good they look together."

He eyed the tray of glassware.

"Yeah, yeah. I know." She hoisted the tray. "You coming out after?"

He shrugged, but Danny was already pushing through to the kitchen. He looked at his watch. An hour to go.

Kate always stopped in the kitchen to say goodnight to the staff after a function, and tonight was no different. He watched her depart, hand-in-hand with her husband, and wished desperately for his other vice.

Satisfied that Margot had a handle on things, he slipped out into the vineyard and down to the dock the owners kept for summer lake traffic.

He let his legs dangle over the edge, lit a cigarette, and listened to Lake Champlain lap at the wood beneath him, knocking his ashes carefully into a paper cup.

He could hear footsteps on the dirt path above. He'd thought the vines hid him from view, but he hadn't counted on Danny..

"Those things are gross. Girls won't want to kiss you."

"Jeez, Danny, are you thirteen?"

"It's a good thing you're grandfathered in. People call me *Danielle* these days." She plunked down next to him. "And I'm twenty-one, as you well know. You were at my birthday party."

She'd thrown back every shot anyone bought her, including an ill-advised round of schnapps. He'd held her hair back while she threw up in the ladies' room, then driven her out to Fuller's Dairy, where she stayed when she was home from school. She'd changed all his radio presets, but she hadn't puked in his car.

"How did you know I was down here?"

She wiggled her fingers like a sideshow mystic. "I see everyyy-thinggg."

"Weirdo." He put out a hand to nudge her, but the playful gesture felt wrong somehow.

"I saw you attempt a subtle exit after Margot clocked us out. When you didn't come back, I figured you were hiding, or you finally drowned yourself because Kate Pease is still married to Mr. Tall Dark And Broody."

"Nice, Danny." He rubbed out the cigarette, dropping the butt into the cup. Burning down his place of employment--or the terraces of Marquette and Frontenac grapes--wasn't on his to-do list for the evening. "Don't you have someone else to torture?"

"Actually, no." She tilted her head and batted her lashes. "And I need a ride."

He sighed. Danielle Beaudette was not a flirt, but her thick, black cat-eye makeup and sooty eyelashes made a convincing argument in her favor nonetheless.

"Come on." He hoisted himself up and grabbed his soaking filter, swimming in its cup. "For all you know, I have a hot date to get to after I drop you off with the cows."

Danny laughed heartily at his back all the way up the hill to the staff parking lot, but she was uncharacteristically quiet during the ride out County Road.

"You okay?"

She tucked her hair behind her ear, her face deeply shadowed in the dark car. "Yeah. Just thinking."

He swung into the Fullers' driveway. The farmhouse was dark, except for a light in the kitchen window.

She gathered up a grimy messenger bag from the floor of his car. "You want to come in? I didn't eat before the party, so I'm going to make some food."

He thought of the older couple who owned the farm. "I don't want to impose."

"Oh, Walt and Molly are next door tonight visiting their grandbaby." She opened the car door, climbed out, then leaned back in. Andy couldn't help appreciating a brief view of unexpected lace and curved flesh. "So?"

He *was* hungry. "Can you cook?"

"Enough to feed myself."

He killed the engine and followed her to the back porch. She fished out keys, let them in, and pointed him to a basket of slippers before unlacing her black combat boots, toeing off her socks, and sliding her feet into a pair of green suede moccasins. "Molly doesn't like shoes in the house."

He poked around until he found slip-on fleece house shoes that sort of fit and shuffled after Danny, through a cozy den and into the kitchen.

Danny was already banging around the kitchen. She'd pulled out a cast iron skillet, some bacon and a loaf of Sweet Pease honey-oat sandwich bread.

"BLTs?"

It struck him as odd, seeing Kate's bread on someone's counter. He'd made countless sandwiches at work over the years, but rarely considered that people who bought whole loaves might do the same.

"Earth to Andy?" Danny rapped on the skillet with a pair of tongs, then waved at him with them. "Can you stop thinking about the boss for four seconds and open that cabinet? Plates."

A violent flush rose up his neck. "I wasn't—"

"Thinking about Kate? Liar. Your face gets all weird when you do." She rolled her eyes back and let her jaw go slack.

He fetched the plates, then reached for the single tomato resting on the windowsill. Danny laid the bacon out in the hot pan, and handed him the serrated knife from the block by the stove top.

He sliced the bread, then the tomato, thick like he would have for a customer. "Toaster?"

Danny kicked at a lower cabinet door. The toaster was inside on a shelf, its cord coiled around it.

He had to cram the bread in a little, but he got the toaster going. Danny was flipping bacon. The kitchen smelled amazing.

Andy opened the fridge, looking for mayonnaise, and found the jar on the door. What interested him more was a stack of glass storage containers. There was a beautiful collection of cheeses in those containers.

"Are we allowed to eat the cheese?"

Danny laughed, pulling the last slice of bacon from the pan. The toast popped. "Yes. Look." She slid the skillet off the burner to cool and wiped her hands on a kitchen towel. "I live here. Walt and Molly stepped in and offered me a place with them when things at home were... not good. This is the place I think of when someone says home. If we want to eat the cheese, we eat the cheese."

While Danny started assembling sandwiches, Andy pulled together a plate of cheeses. He glanced back at Danny, who had laid the sandwiches out open faced. "Where's the lettuce?"

"Still in the garden."

She picked up the plate with the sandwiches, reached into the fridge for a glass bottle of milk, and breezed past him.

"Where are you going?"

"Bring the cheese. We're going to get the lettuce."

He tromped after her, delayed by changing back into his shoes.

Her slippers lay abandoned by the door, but so too were her heavy, black boots.

He'd expected a practical vegetable patch. Instead, Danny waited for him on a whimsical bench fashioned from what looked like driftwood, amidst a maze of trellises and raised beds. A lush jungle of edibles slept in the blue darkness. Andy smelled damp earth and growing things.

He recognized Danny in that scent. This garden, it was hers.

"You got any basil out here?"

She laughed, pointing to a nested stack of round pots. "Over there. Top tier."

He wound his way between the beds. Pea vines, leafy bean bushes, and taller climbing squashes, blossoms closed against the night. Flowers were artfully tucked in with the food.

"Did you do all this?"

Danny's voice floated back to him. "Sort of. There's always been a kitchen garden here. Since before Walt was born. He and Molly have helped me with building the boxes and stuff, but yeah. It's what I do, or at least what I want to do."

He often forgot that about her, since he only saw her at work, or when the Sweet Pease gang went out after hours. She'd worked at Coulson's nursery, too, before starting college, and still did in the summers. He pinched off a handful of sweet basil leaves and brought them back to her on the cheese plate.

"Better than plain old lettuce."

She shook the dew off the leaves and spread them on the sandwiches, patting the bench next to her. Her feet were bare, toes curling into the stone and dust.

It was only just dark enough for stars thanks to the late summer sunset. He let the living quiet settle over him while he tucked in. The valley chorused with peeper frogs and crickets, the occasional car or truck on County Road, and the barely perceptible sleep-sounds of the dairy herd.

"You were right about the basil." Danny set down what remained of her sandwich, and scooped up a bit of soft cheese with her finger. "I hope you don't mind my fingers in the food."

He didn't, now that she mentioned it. "We did eat unwashed basil."

"Unwashed basil, fingers in the cheese. We are adventurers." She licked her finger. "That's really good."

He didn't want to be intrigued by her bowed lips, her fine-boned hands that were always slightly chapped, at odds with her pin-up girl makeup and ever-changing hair.

"I've been paying attention to the vendors."

"Impressive, since Kate's usually around for that."

He set his plate down too hard, nearly sending his half-eaten sandwich into the gravel path. "You never let up. What is it to you if I like Kate?"

She leaned back and leveled him with a cool look that reminded him that she wasn't just the sarcastic kid Margot had hired a couple of years back. "Maybe I don't want to see you miss opportunities while you're pining for someone who is never going to feel that way about you."

"Yeah," his laugh turned bitter. "Like who? It's not like I've ever been a girl magnet."

Danny pursed her lips—with a healthy dose of side-eye—and returned to eating her sandwich, snagging a slice of another cheese and sliding it between the bread slices as she did.

Andy left his food, the bench, and Danny's infuriating snark and wandered into her garden. Through the fir stand ahead, he could make out the shadowed silhouette of the grand Victorian house next door. Around a corner of the building, he could just see the flickering glow of firelight, and if he stretched out his ears, he could hear laughter and low music.

Kate—and her husband—might very well be there. The owners were her friends.

"I lived there for a while when I was younger."

Danny's voice was soft—wistful—and he felt sorry for taking a verbal swing at her.

"I didn't know that."

"My mom was Meg Swift's home health aide before they moved to be closer to her grown kids. They let us stay in the apartment over the garage." He hadn't heard her get up, but she appeared next to him among her plants. "I was always happy there. I mean, I was a teenage jerk to my mom, and I had stupid taste in boys, but things didn't get bad until we moved in with my uncle."

Andy slung an arm around her, hugging her to his side. "You seem happy here, though."

She shifted slightly, leaning into him a little. He liked the way she fit there.

"I am. I have better taste in men now, too."

He wondered who the lucky guy was just as he realized he was holding another guy's girl, then let his arm drop away.

"You're not even going to ask."

He turned at the sharp wonder he heard. Her expression was fierce, her body suddenly rigid with tension.

"You, you idiot."

Him, what? He had just enough time to blink before she stretched up and kissed him full on the mouth. She let her lips linger for a beat against his; his body responded before his head could catch up.

He caught her arms, sliding his hands down to hold her hands, leaning in to let the kiss play out between them.

She tasted of basil leaves. Her skin was impossibly soft, right down to her palms, but he could feel the calluses on her fingers. The scent of earth and rain clung to her like perfume.

She rocked back on her heels, pulling away from him, but holding him in her gaze. "You."

He reached up to touch her cheek and she pressed her face into his hand. The gesture was so unabashedly tender, so unlike Danny. A pang of longing squeezed his chest.

"I didn't know." He whispered it, feeling every inch the idiot she'd called him.

Danny tightened her hold on his other hand. "Now you do."

～

Cameron D. Garriepy
A Thornton Vermont Story
SUGARING SEASON

Sugaring season is the season when you tap the trees for sugar that turns into maple syrup. I've married someone from Vermont, so it's an expression I kept hearing, and I'm like, 'What is that? That's just so beautiful.' I like the idea it's the very, very first murmurings of spring.

~ Beth Orton

SUGARING SEASON

The house was too big.

It had been too big for years, but for one art teacher staring down her retirement years, it was cavernous.

Rosie had dialed the numbers of all three of Thornton's real estate agents in the month since her dad's funeral, but hung up before anyone could answer the calls. Generations of her family history—generations of Thornton's history, some might argue—were woven into the framing of the Cartwright family's house on Chapel Street.

Surely someone would want it when she was gone?

With that grim thought for company, she shrugged into her late-husband's barn coat and stepped out onto the the front porch. A thin, dirty coating of old snow and sandy muck took the shine off a water-color day.

From the top of the steps she could see both the town common and the end of the street, where a muddy footpath wound down to a broad bend in the Thorn River. Every March an uncertain spring came like clockwork—mud season—and every year save the handful she and Tim had lived somewhere else, this had been her view.

Next door, John Pease was clearing winter's debris from the flag-stone walkway between their porch and the sidewalk, pausing to clear the wet, brown patches where the first tightly furled emergences of his wife Cora's perennials were pushing up through the soil, a surer sign that spring would come—in its own time—than any Rosie knew.

Cora waved from her steps, where she waited with her walking stick. John saw his wife wave and paused to lean on his broom handle.

"Morning, Rose."

Rosie and John had known one another all their lives, growing up side-by-side in houses their families had owned since the end of the Civil War. Rosie raised a hand in greeting to them both. "Morning. On your way out?"

Cora rapped her cane against the railing. "The boss says I need a walk before we drive down to Rutland for my appointment."

"The boss takes his orders from the doctor," John said to his wife. He pushed a stray twig off the walkway with one foot, then turned to Rosie. "What's got you up and out so early today?"

"Taking flatlanders for tap-line tours."

"Sugaring season already? It was just Christmas a few days ago, wasn't it?" John took in the gently undulating grays of the sky overhead. "Nice day for it."

"Do you want to stop by for supper?" Cora added. "Katie and Jack are coming by. The whole gang will be here. We'd love to have you."

Grandchildren. Rosie sucked in a breath to cool the hot pinch of regret in her chest. "I think I'll be worn right out after spending the day in the sugarbush, and I've got to be at the school tomorrow to start setting up the fifth grade art show."

The fifth grade at the school named for her mother. Another legacy like a stone around her neck.

Twin waves of loss and unanswered prayers swamped her, but she steadied herself and offered her neighbors a smile. Rosie Cartwright Keller had places to be, and her sorrows weren't invited.

Tommy Napoli gazed across a white field studded with tidy rows of Fraser fir saplings. Fingers of pink-gold sunrise touched the tops of the maple trees all around him, and a fine mist hung over the shallow bowl in the landscape that formed West's Tree Farm.

His first thought was that the Lake Champlain Valley could make a poet out of anyone. His second was that he'd have to find a poetic way to tell his only daughter she was out of the will.

His alarm had gone off at 4 a.m., rousing him to a freezing room in a foursquare cabin and a twenty yard hike through a crust of late-winter snow to stand in line for the outhouse. That was three hours ago. His belly might be full of pancakes and maple syrup, strong coffee, and thick-cut bacon, but his back was sore, his toes were icy, and the sun was just barely up.

"It'll be so cool, Dad," Kayla had said when he'd opened his Christmas gift three months before. "Three days on a working farm, *making* maple syrup!"

So far they'd met with the owner and learned the terminology, then toured the sugarbush, following the pipelines that webbed the forest with tubes that carried the tree sap to collection vats. He had to admit, it was interesting. He'd never considered the labor involved, that ten gallons of the clear running sap produced about a quart of the sweet stuff.

He trudged along, caught between uncertainty about the whole *staycation* concept—Kayla's word, not his—and a kind of cautious delight at his surroundings. He'd never spent much time in the woods. As one of six working guests on the farm property, he'd experienced more rural life in the twelve hours since check in than he had his entire life.

The guide was a guy probably twenty years his junior who'd grown up there, with a name like a soap opera millionaire. Sterling led them on through the trees. "We're going to head down to the sugar-house now, to learn about the evaporation process."

Tommy could see clouds of steam billowing from beyond a rise in the forest floor. There was a faint sweetness on the air, and despite the breakfast he'd shared with his cohort, his stomach rumbled in response.

A different, larger group was assembled near the path that wound up from the parking lot, each clutching a pamphlet and a small galvanized bucket. Sterling waved to a woman waiting by the sugarhouse door.

She looked up from her clipboard and Tommy's chest tightened with something like... lust. It had been so long since he'd felt it, he barely recognized it. She had a lean, ropy build, and a long chestnut braid shot through with streaks of almost pure white. He'd read the term "heart-shaped" face before, but had never thought of it as something an actual person had before this morning. Her smile was generous, her eyes welcoming. He'd never been good at guessing a woman's age, but he thought maybe she wasn't too much younger than he was.

"Morning, Sterling," she called out. "That your new crop of guests?"

"And fine recruits they are." Sterling addressed the waiting group. "Folks, you lucked out. Rosie's my favorite tour guide."

"You say that to all of us." The woman—Rosie—blushed; there was familiar affection in her small head shake. "Enjoy your stay, folks."

Sterling saluted the woman and led them away from the tour group, but Tommy glanced back twice at her through the gilded steam, just to see the first light on her profile.

Rosie was just about to leave when Tony West found her. Uncle to the current owners of the farm and resident codger and dogsbody, Tony was also tasked with handling the working guests.

"Oh, I love my Rosie child." He sang as he jogged the dirt path from the sugarhouse to the parking lot. "She got the way to make me happy."

"What's up, Tony?" Rosie pocketed the keys to her Subaru. "Besides Neil Diamond?"

Tony's eyes twinkled. "Can't an old man ask a pretty girl to stay on and volunteer her Saturday night entertaining a bunch of tourists?"

Pretty girl hardly suited. Nearly sixty, formerly sturdy, now lean to the point of stringiness, never the bombshell her mother had been,

Rosie had taken after her grandmother Eolia—a handsome woman, folks'd said. Tim had always liked what he'd seen, anyway.

Tim, like her parents, was gone, so what did it matter?

"Flattery will get you a lot of places, but not tonight." She laughed to soften the blow, but she hadn't entirely lied to her neighbors. She wasn't feeling up for company.

Tony rested his butt on the hood of her Crosstrek and ticked off the names of every West who might have saved her from volunteering.

"Junior—sorry, Sterling—and Miss Ivy have plans tonight, and Jasper and two of the little ones are laid up with late-season flu. Lorelei is up to her neck in fevers and snot. There's no one else but us."

She'd tramped the trails that wound through the sugarbush six times, chatting with visitors to the farm about sugaring and taps and life in Vermont. Her throat was dry, her quads weary. The last thing she wanted was to serve a family-style dinner at the main house, or to grease social wheels for the work-stay group gathering around the fireplace.

Ignoring her wants, she pulled out her keys. "I'll bring the car around to the big house."

Tony pushed his rump off the hood. "I'll meet you. Gotta swing by the bunkhouse first and gather the troops."

Rosie climbed into the car, leaning back against the headrest and watching Tony trot off. She couldn't even be angry with him; he was that charming.

She started the car and drove the half mile of mud road through the Christmas tree meadows. The Wests' farmhouse now served not only as Jasper and Lorelei West's home, but also the headquarters for their agri-tourism ventures.

Lorelei, pale and harried, met her in the kitchen. "You're a gem, Rosie. Thank you."

Rosie hung her coat on a peg by the door. "What's on the menu?"

"Nothing fancy." Lorelei peered into the oven—an ancient wood-fired Aga—and tidied a row of Pyrex dishes covered in foil. "There's a lasagna in there, and everything else is ready to serve."

Tony stumped in. "Nothing I can't handle."

The work-stay guests followed. Rosie counted them as they trailed Tony through the door. Two younger couples, a lean, tanned woman in expensive activewear, and a guy about her own age.

Lorelei leaned in to whisper in Rosie's ear. "I'll skedaddle. I need to check on the kids. And Jasper."

"Night, Lore." Tony took off his knit hat, waving it at the group behind him before shoving it in his coat pocket. "Rosie, this is Karen and Doug from Stamford, Jana and Brian from Atlanta, Hazel from Los Angeles, and Tom from Boston."

Rosie slipped into hospitality mode; her weariness could wait. "Pleasure to meet you all. I hope you're enjoying your stay so far. Go on in and have a seat in the dining room. Tony and I will get dinner on the table. There's wine and soft drinks on the sideboard."

Tom from Boston was the last to walk past her. "Rosie." He nodded in greeting, the corners of his eyes crinkling when he smiled.

He had beautiful eyes, dappled gold and earthy brown. Beautiful, and lonely. Maybe it was the aching loneliness in her own reflection that imagined what she saw in his casual expression, or maybe it was the way this man's smile recalled her father's. She'd have staked the house on Chapel Street that Tom from Boston had lost someone, too.

Tommy watched her over the course of the meal. In the arc of her shoulders and the way her smile sometimes faltered, he could see how tired she was and how well she held it all inside. She passed trays of food, refilled glasses, and made conversation with practiced ease, but he felt it in his bones when their eyes met down the table.

She was bone weary and sad.

When the group retired to the living room, where seats were arranged around the broad flagstone hearth, Tommy waited until Rosie sat to approach her.

"Can I get you anything?"

"Oh, no. I'm fine." She'd answered on autopilot. He recognized the tendency and waited it out, gratified when she changed her mind. "Actually, I'd really like some sparkling water. It's in the wine fridge." She gestured to a large cabinet in one corner that disguised a miniature bar area.

Tony was setting up teams for Scrabble when he got back. "Cracklin' Rose, you in?"

"I'll man the dictionary." Rosie took her phone out of her pocket, then looked at Tommy. "Do you play?"

"I was never much for board games. Too restless."

"My father was an English teacher. Impossible to beat." She lit up at the mention of her father.

"Did you always live here?"

She laughed. "You won't believe it. I live in the house I grew up in. My dad's great-grandfather built it. My family's owned that lot since they turned up here after the Civil War."

"No shit?" Tommy leaned in. Some of the sorrow had lifted when she talked about her family, and he wanted to see if he could keep it at bay. Tommy hadn't wanted to kiss a woman so badly since… *Sorry, Ell.*

If his dead wife heard him, she didn't reply.

"How about you?" Rosie asked, settling into her chair. "In my experience, no one who's *from* Boston ever actually lives *in* Boston."

"Got me." The warmth of shared humor flowed through his veins. "Medford, born and bred, but you can see the city from the back deck of my parents' apartment. My dad ran a convenience store once he settled down. He came from somewhere out west, came to Boston after he got out of the Navy to live with some cousins. By the time I came along, he owned the building I grew up in, and two others on the street."

"My dad was in the Navy, too. Korea." Rosie tilted her glass; the carbonation rolled in the water. "I used to dream about growing up in the city. Running on the sidewalks, the noise, the crowds. I thought it would be just like West Side Story." The sadness veiled her expression again. "My mom loved musicals."

Grief is like a pickpocket, Tommy thought. The moment you're distracted, it slips sticky fingers into your heart and steals your joy. A little bit at a time, here and there, when you're not paying attention.

"*West Side Story* it was not. My neighborhood was more like *Moonstruck*." He let himself drift back to his childhood for a moment, the block of triple deckers that rubbed up against the university, the festivals in the North End with his vast tribe of cousins. "Or maybe the Prince Spaghetti ad."

"Anthonnnnyyyy!" Rosie sing-songed.

She'd nailed it. Tommy laughed. "Pretty much. I had a Nonna who lived on the third floor around the corner from Paul Revere's house; she could holler down any kid halfway to Southie."

"Neither of my grandmothers ever hollered." Rosie's eyes misted over, and her gaze dropped toward the fizz rising to the top of her drink.

Tommy saw the humor she'd tried for and desperately wanted to bring her back from whatever memory clouded her eyes. "I met Ellen at the Feast of Saint Somebody-or-other back in 1980. She was at Wellesley. Way out of my league, that's about as *West Side Story* as it got."

"She's your wife?" Rosie's voice was husky.

"Was. Yeah. Died a year ago. Two kids, grown now. I miss her like hell most times."

Where the hell had that come from? Guilt bubbled up in his belly. What business did he have, coaxing smiles from a beautiful woman by firelight when the memory of his wife still shot through him like an electrocution?

Rosie's head tilted and she set her glass down. "She was a lucky woman."

"I was the lucky one." He cleared his throat. "Is there a lucky man waiting for you to come home?"

Rosie's wobbly laugh didn't ring true. "I've been on my own for a while now."

"I'm sorry."

A log on the fire popped, and Tommy realized that the rest of the room, with their small talk and Scrabble, had faded while he fell under Rosie's spell. A spell she had no idea she was casting.

"Rose, you ready?" Tony looked up from the board, where he and Hazel from California were teamed over their tiles. "The Southerners are trying to tell me that's a word."

Hazel was subtly shaking her head. Rosie squinted at the board. Jana from Atlanta pointed to QUIXOTRY. Tony was grinning like a fool.

"I think they're right, Tony." Her practiced social graces covered her face like a veil. "I wouldn't challenge."

"Oh, all right." Tony's good ol' boy charm was in full-effect. Which was, Tommy figured, part of the reason Tony handled the work-stay groups.

Tommy leaned in to look at the board, then looked back at Rosie. "If I didn't know better, I'd say you and Tony had a routine."

This time when Rosie smiled, there was a playful twinkle in her eye. "Maybe."

"This is real neat. The way they've set all this up," he said. "I couldn't imagine before I got here how it would be."

"A lot of it was Sterling's idea," Rosie replied.

"So, how did you get involved?"

"I volunteered." She laughed, the veil dropping again as she relaxed. "I've been buying syrup here for years. I was up here one day a few years ago, and Lorelei—that's Jasper's wife—was talking about starting this up, and wondering how they were going to manage. I offered to help."

"So, you and Tony aren't..." Tommy hoped he sounded casual.

"No." Rosie giggled into her sparkling water. "He's practically old enough to be my father. Though I suppose at our age... I haven't... there hasn't been..."

Uncertainty settled in again as she trailed off.

"Me neither," he replied, then cast around for a new topic. It was too soon to tell her he'd been considering just that since the moment he'd laid eyes on her. "Do you work here full-time?"

"No. I'm an art teacher down in Thornton. At the primary school. I had both Jasper and Sterling as students when they were kids."

"That's pretty cute."

"They were pretty cute, but don't let Sterling hear that."

The couple from Connecticut cheered. Rosie looked at the board. They'd just set down their last tile.

"Let's tally the scores," Tony said. "Winners get out of dish duty at breakfast."

While the players did their math, Tony raised his beer in Rosie's direction. "Easy night to be the arbiter, Rosie child."

Rosie lifted her glass in reply. "Always a pleasure."

"Well, kids," Tony continued. "I'd suggest hitting your bunks. Wake up call is at 4 tomorrow morning."

"I should be getting on my way, too," Rosie said. "It's been really nice talking to you, Tom."

He stood when Rosie did, unsure of how to say goodnight to her, frightened to let her go. They were strangers, but somehow not.

"Tommy." He offered her his hand, wishing they weren't surrounded by people. "My friends call me Tommy."

"Goodnight, Tommy." Her hand was cool and soft in his, and he convinced himself her fingers lingered against his palm when she turned to go. "I hope you enjoy the rest of your stay."

Rosie's heart fluttered all the way back to town. The girlish feeling embarrassed her, even as she craved more. Tommy from Medford had woken something in her, running like sap in her cold, dormant heart.

Pulling into her driveway, she shook her head to clear it, to no avail.

He had competent hands and a nice jaw. Funny the things she noticed after ignoring that part of living for so long. Not that she'd been looking, but he filled out the seat of his jeans nicely, without much belly over his belt—a bonus in men of a certain age.

Not that she should be complaining. She grimaced at her reflection in the front door glass. The cold porch light was no friend of hers. She looked a fright.

She couldn't recall the last time she'd flirted. Before Tim got sick, probably. Tony West didn't count.

The lights were all on next door. She felt a pang of guilt at refusing the invitation from the Peases, then staying late at West's.

You are a grown woman. They didn't give it a second thought.

Rosie did give the evening a second thought, and then a third. She couldn't get Tommy out of her head. The way he'd looked at her. His evident enjoyment of the people and circumstances he was in. It wasn't often anymore that she saw her life through fresh eyes.

She locked the front door and turned out the porch light, pressing the button on her key fob one last time to make sure the car was locked. It would be just like her to leave it unlocked for the first time since she'd started the practice, and all because she'd spent the whole drive home imagining romantic feelings in a man she'd likely never see again.

A man whose amber-flecked eyes remained her of the West's Farm syrup she took home in mason jars as payment for tour-guiding in the sugarbush.

Tommy fell into bed exhausted within moments of returning from the big house. Hazel and the two couples were embroiled in a discussion of syrup grades and what it cost to get the good stuff where they lived; it was all Tommy could do to keep his head upright.

Despite a shower before dinner and the hint of woodsmoke on his shirt, Tommy could still smell the sap on his skin. He'd made a habit— since Ellen died—of cataloguing his day before he slept. Proof on the worst days that he was still alive.

Sterling had split them up into teams, and they'd rotated through the different areas of the sugaring operation throughout the day. Tommy had enjoyed the ferocious heat of the evaporation tanks, the sweet rushing steam and the quiet company of Sterling's father and uncle Tony. The two men talked about diversifying small farms, tradition, and innovative revenue streams. They didn't ask personal questions; Tommy didn't offer much.

The work day had ended, in anticipation of a pleasant evening with his fellow guests before turning in early.

Until Rosie.

He'd thought her lovely, waiting outside the sugarhouse in her practical coat and boots. Inside, warm by the fire and full of good food and a glass of wine, he found her intoxicating. So much so, he'd babbled about his childhood. And Ellen.

His cheeks went hot at the memory, but he couldn't think how he would have spoken differently. Rosie didn't strike him as the small-talk type.

She'd gone away somewhere at the mention of the North End, somewhere important, judging by the sparkle of tears she'd blinked away.

He laid in the bottom bunk, staring at the wire mesh that cradled the empty mattress above him, breathing in the mingled scents of old timbers and laundry soap from his sheets. His roommate—Hazel, the woman from California—came in a few minutes later, disappearing behind an old-fashioned boudoir screen before crawling into the bottom bunk across the room in a tank top and flannel pajama pants.

"Night, Tom."

He hadn't slept in a room with another human since the night Ellen passed. A year and six days later, there were two women in the room: Hazel, and Rosie.

She didn't need to be up early, but Rosie was awake with the sun. The green of spring was in the milder air and a pale azure sky was rising over the mountain range when she walked out to get the local paper from her walkway.

The custodial staff wouldn't open the school until ten. Plenty of time to offer Lorelei a hand with breakfast at the big house.

She was young enough at heart to have embraced texting, and a quick exchange confirmed that she could be useful.

Do you mind meeting Tony at the sugarhouse to collect them in the truck?

No. No, she didn't mind at all, Rosie thought with a smile.

She was humming Neil Diamond as she started her car, but it was Tommy Napoli's maple sugar eyes she was seeing.

Tommy finally decided not to disown his daughter at all somewhere between the fifth and six bucket of sap he emptied on the second morning. He and Hazel were checking a cluster of outlying trees that were still tapped the old way, with buckets that required checking.

As much as he liked the innovation of vacuum osmosis drawing the sap down the lines to collection vats, this felt like the kind of connection to food and work that Kayla had waxed on about while he puzzled over her unexpected gift.

"You haven't gone farther than the store or the office since mom died."

He'd looked to her older brother for help, but Zach was no help. "Dad, you're turning into a fossil."

"Mom would be so mad." Unshed tears glittered in his daughter's eyes, despite the sass, and a lump rose in his throat.

Tommy had capitulated. "I bet it'll be great."

He was tired and sore, he'd forgotten how to eat big meals in company, and he'd be glad as hell to get back to indoor plumbing, but he'd never in a million years have chosen this adventure for himself, and it *was* great.

"What were you and Rosie talking about last night? Do you two know each other?" Hazel stopped to re-tie her boots.

"Just conversation," he muttered, cursing the fierce rush of embarrassed color in his face. It was difficult to meet her eyes, but he made himself.

Hazel had a dazzling smile. "I know *just conversation*, honey, and that wasn't it."

"I met her yesterday, same as you."

Hazel picked up her sap buckets and started back down the path, giving him a coy glance over one shoulder. "She's cute."

There was nothing safe to say there, so Tommy chose silence.

"I write, you know," Hazel said without turning. "For TV. I know talking and behavior and words."

"Anything I'd know?"

She listed off one show he'd heard of, and a few he was sure Kayla and Zach would know. His attempts to keep it casual were thwarted. Hazel was direct to the point of pain. "She liked you, but here's the thing: if you were my characters, I'd have you as people who went way back, but maybe lost each other and were just rediscovering something. You were a pretty picture there by the fireplace."

She didn't seem to require a response, so Tommy only followed.

The sugarhouse came into view over the next rise of blue spruce— these trees looked like they were nearly ready for sleigh rides and families in matching parkas.

"Well, I'll be damned." Hazel had a commanding laugh.

Tommy squinted to see what his roommate was so delighted by, and this time the punch of desire was clear and immediate. Rosie, her long hair wrapped up in a loose bun, leggings and less sturdy boots peeking out from under a long, puffy coat, was leaning by the door.

Rosie looked up at the sound of Hazel's laughter, and he picked up the pace to get to her sooner.

She straightened at his approach.

"Hey there, Rosie."

"Tommy." His name sounded like home when she said it. He hadn't had it this bad since Ellen had cut in front of him in the gelato line all those years ago.

Hazel, who'd already been inside with her buckets, sidled up and took his from his hands without asking, tossing him a significant glance before vanishing inside the sugarhouse again.

"I've been out on the buckets since dawn." He felt, as Kayla would say, *lame* just saying it.

Rosie brightened. "You sound like you've been doing this all your life."

"Not bad," he chuckled, happy she hadn't noticed his unease, "for a guy who mostly pushes invoices and purchase orders all day."

"For the moment," Rosie countered, "you're going to do some light food service work."

"Am I?" He realized with a little zing that Rosie was flirting with him.

"I'm supposed to collect you all for breakfast, but I'm early, so you and I can head up to the Big House early and finish putting the meal together for Lorelei. I'll leave the truck here for Tony and the others to follow us."

"That sounds great."

"What do you that you push purchase orders all day?" Rosie asked. The trail from the sugar house to the West's home led through the pumpkin fields—or what would be the pumpkin fields, Tony had told them, since this time of year, they were sleeping.

The sap was the first thing to wake up, Tony said. Then the mud.

Tommy liked the neat furrows where last year's crop of Halloween jack-o-lanterns had grown.

"A lumber yard. Nothing fancy. Local place that mostly sells to contractors. Not one of those box stores. Got a job there when I was a kid, moved up. It was steady work. Now I handle a lot of the mill contracts."

Rosie watched his face when he talked. He'd missed that, having someone really listen. Kayla and Zach were good kids; he loved when they came around, but they were caught up in being young. He missed Ellen's half of the conversation as much as he'd missed her laughter in the kitchen and her body next to his in their bed.

"And you've got kids. Where are they?" She didn't look at him when she asked about them. She'd said she didn't have kids. Tommy wondered if she regretted that.

"My girl Kayla has a job in Boston." He flashed her a smile. "She doesn't live there, either."

They passed the walk through the fallow pumpkin patch while Tommy told Rosie about Kayla's work and Zach's new wife. They reached the yard that surrounded the Big House, and Rosie stopped at a sap bucket looped around the gatepost. She scooped out a handful of small brown pellets and scattered them for the chickens milling around the yard.

The hens flocked around Rosie's feet. "I just love them. They're so silly."

"They seem to like you a lot, too." He'd never felt kinship with chickens before that morning.

"They like the feed." She offered him a palmful. "They'll like you, too."

Rosies's chilly fingers brushed his as she transferred the chicken feed to his cupped hand. Tommy scattered it, grinning at the way the hens bobbed and pecked for their treats.

"See?" she said. "They like you."

But do you, Rosie? He fell into step with her and they crossed the lawn together, leaving the chickens to their food.

Tommy knew his way around a kitchen, it seemed.

Even after thirty years of marriage, Tim couldn't do more than boil water and grill a steak; the subtler arts of pots, pans, knives, ingredients—those were a foreign language he'd left for Rosie to translate.

She'd set Tommy to scrambling eggs while she sliced a loaf of Lorelei's homemade sandwich bread for toasting. There were warm spiced apples and fresh maple butter for the toast, and an urn of coffee huddled warmly on the sideboard.

Tommy scraped eggs into the chafing dish Rosie'd left for him. "I'll take these to the table. Can I get anything while I'm over there?"

"Bring back the creamer and sugar bowl to refill?" She asked the question with the kind of idle familiarity she might've used with Tony, or Tim before he'd passed, and it put a hitch in her slicing rhythm to consider it.

He was gone long enough to draw her attention from the food. She found him in the dining room, looking at an old photograph on the wall where Jasper and Lorelei had created a gallery of the farm's history to watch over their guests.

"Is that you?" He asked without turning, and Rosie knew right away which photo he meant.

It was her, with her parents and brother, on a winter hayride. The Wests in those days had been Jasper's grandparents, and it had been a working farm, with the trees on the side in December.

"Yeah." She picked up the creamer and sugar bowl. "My parents were some of the first people to come here for Christmas trees."

"Your mom was a knockout." When he turned to her, his eyes were warm, wanting. "You take after her around the eyes."

Without warning, Rosie set down the dishes she'd been holding. She'd thought she was ready for a little flirt, a little bit of the weightless carousel whirl of desire and anticipation, but this was too much of not enough.

He couldn't know that summoning her mother's frustrating, beloved ghost, with her ingenue eyes and Monroe hips would bring Rosie's reckless confidence crashing down. She wasn't a knockout. She wasn't her mother.

She was reliable, just a little sad, but not enough to make people uncomfortable. *Poor Rosie*, she imagined them saying, *but she soldiers on.*

Tony barged into the kitchen, with the others in tow, and Rosie took her chance. "Tony's here. He'll get you through breakfast. Thanks for doing the eggs."

She grabbed her coat from the hook where she'd left it, and dashed across the yard, scattering the chickens in her path, wishing she'd hadn't left her car by the sugar house, cursing herself for a sentimental fool.

～

"Rosie? Are you okay?" Gail Swanson, fifth grade teacher and her dear friend for years, planted herself in front of Rosie, hands on hips.

"What? Yes," Rosie said. "Of course. Why?"

"You've been half a world away all day."

Rosie paused, looking critically at the pair of clay pots in her hands. She couldn't exactly say why she had those two in particular, or where she'd been going with them when Gail interrupted.

"You wouldn't believe me if I told you."

Gail took the two pieces and set them down in front of two Impressionist copies from the unit on Monet. "Try me. We'll walk over to the farmer's market and get a snack and some fresh air while you tell me what's going on."

Better to walk with Gail than drift through the tangled forest of grief in her heart.

It was still cold, but the air was mild, the first kiss of spring the weak sunlight. Halfway between the school and the common, Rosie drew in a lungful. "You know I work sugaring season up at West's."

She knew Gail knew, so Rosie went on.

"I was up there yesterday, and Tony drafted me to help out with the work-stay crew dinner. Jasper and the kids have the flu."

"Poor Lorelei."

They shared a pitying smile for Jasper's wife.

"I ended up talking to a man from outside of Boston for a while after dinner—" She saw Gail's brows shoot up, and interrupted. "He was nice, and lonely. He's there alone. Stop."

"It's been six years since you lost Tim." Gail reached for her hand. "It would be okay for you to have talked to a nice man for no reason at all except that you wanted to."

The farmer's market was never crowded in March, and the sparse attendance generally thinned out by midday, so Rosie and Gail had their pick of what remained. Sweet Pease Bakery ran a coffee and pastry cart, so they headed there first.

Coffee and danishes in hand, they were choosing a bench when Rosie heard her name.

Tommy Napoli, wearing a West's Tree Farm ball cap, came around the table of maple themed goods the farm sent down most Sundays. "Hi."

He took off his hat, clutching it between his hands, and glancing back at the table and his whip-thin, yoga-toned companion. "Hazel and I got the farmer's market shift. When I saw you, I had to--" He seemed to realize Gail was with her and stopped to offer her a handshake. "Tommy Napoli."

"Gail Swanson. Pleasure to meet you."

Rosie saw mischief in her friend's eyes and quelled it with a look. "Gail and I teach at the primary school. Tom is a work-stay guest at West's this weekend."

"Could I just..." *Consternation.* That was the word for his expression. "Could we talk a minute?"

Gail perked up, beaming at Rosie. "I'm going to go have a look at what's left in Fuller's cheese case. Catch me up when you're ready to head back."

They were barely alone before Tommy spoke. "I swear, I don't know what I said this morning that hurt you. I wish you hadn't gone." His accent broadened when he was riled up. His dropped r's and broad vowels inspired the same tenderness she'd felt for him by the fireplace the night before. "I didn't mean to come up here and stir up anything. My daughter Kayla planned everything."

"So you said." Rosie hid the enormity of her feelings behind a sip of coffee.

"I might have come up here and gone home without even knowing you existed." He rushed on. "But I— I'm glad I didn't."

"I'm glad, too." The gladness was a warmth just behind her breastbone. Akin to the beating wings of anxiety that had carried her since her husband's death, but welcome. Gentle.

Tommy was all she could see; she couldn't have torn her gaze from his if the farmer's market were burning around them. He brought her hand up to cradle her jaw. His palm was warm. She liked the slight roughness of his skin against her cheek.

When he touched his lips to hers, the entire common might as well have gone up in flames. Everything vanished around them. Her eyes fluttered closed and she leaned into his hand, letting the contact linger. What remained of her rational thoughts told her it wasn't possible that he smelled of maple sugar, but still the sweetness swirled in her nose.

It was Tommy who ended what he'd begun, though his thumb still traced the hollow of her cheek. Her eyes drifted open to him, watching her for... approval? Permission?

"Oh," was all she could say. Wide-eyed and dumbstruck like a girl.

The chuckle rumbled up from his chest in counterpoint to the applause building up around them.

"Tommy!" His work-stay partner whooped from her spot behind their table. Rosie could hear Gail's laughter from somewhere nearby, but all she wanted was to stay close to Tommy long enough to see if this all wasn't a fever dream.

"I'm supposed to leave tomorrow morning." He spoke quietly now, just for the two of them. "But I'd like to stop in town for a bit, maybe have lunch with you." A crooked smile deepened the wrinkles around his mouth. "Maybe kiss you again."

Reality kicked in, reminding her what she was meant to be doing, even as the heat pooling in her belly reacted to the idea of kissing him again. "I teach. Art. I'm an art teacher at the primary school. I have to work."

"I took the whole day off to drive home." His expression clouded. "You know I don't have anyone waiting there. Maybe after the school day?"

"Yes. I supervise the Kindergarten walkers—the little ones who have someone walking to pick them up. Then I'm done. I could meet you—"

"Wherever." He turned, grabbed a pamphlet and the newsletter sign-up pen from his table, and carefully printed his phone number. "You can call, or text. Tell me where to be."

She took the brochure from his hands, feeling the magic start to slip away. Gail had drifted closer, the crowd seemed to have forgotten them. Rosie knew there would be a little talk. Thornton was too small to avoid gossip entirely.

"I will." Rosie reached up to cover Tommy's hand with hers, to reclaim a little of the enchantment. A happy thrill ran down her spine, and she closed her eyes one more time, the better to memorize the way he looked before they parted.

She and Gail were barely out of earshot when Gail looked back at Tommy. "Now you really have to finish that story." She leaned in close. "I don't think anyone's ever watched me walk away the way that man is watching you right now." Gail sighed. "Like the world will end when you disappear."

"We only talked." Rosie kept her eyes on the last bend in the road before the school. Better to imagine such longing. The more distance that stretched out between them, the less possible it all seemed.

Tommy didn't know about lions or lambs, but March in Vermont was *some* kind of changeable creature. After the farmer's market—and he had to admit, his perception of the weather was tangled in the warmth of Rosie's lips—they'd returned to the farm for a sunny afternoon exploring the farm's other aspects: Christmas trees, chickens, a pumpkin patch, and a horse-drawn wagon for hayrides.

By sunset, though, the air stilled. Without the sun, a chill dipped its fingers under his collar.

He'd waited all afternoon for his phone to chirp, but it stayed stubbornly silent in his coat pocket. Night came on, and with it the closing evening activities at the farm. He joined his fellow guests for another farm-to-table meal, this time followed by sugar-on-snow and a starlit hayride through the forested acres.

Hazel snugged herself in next to him, reclining against a hay bale and chafing her hands together while she held her compostable bowl of sticky, fresh syrup cooling on its mound of finely shaved ice between her knees.

"I can't *believe* you kissed her in the middle of the farmer's market. I'm so using that in a script someday."

"Change my name, okay?" Tommy looked sideways at his roommate. "I've got kids and neighbors."

"You're adorable. I'm so glad I came on this trip." She dug into the taffy-like dessert. "My sister sent me. She said I needed to get out of California for five minutes."

Tommy set his own empty bowl in the hay at his feet as they rumbled along. "Never been."

"To California? Oh, you should come visit me."

"Tell you what. I'll come out there when I retire, and you can introduce me to some TV stars."

She shoved his shoulder playfully. "You got it. I'll show you all the good spots." Her smile turned up at one corner. "Maybe you'll bring Rosie along."

"If she calls at all." Tommy couldn't keep the regret out of his voice, and he hated himself for it.

"Keep the faith, Tom." She laid her cheek companionably on his shoulder, sighing up at the starry indigo expanse, softened by feathery moon-silver clouds. "If this sky can exist, there are definitely miracles."

All day, Rosie walked a winding route around the tables in the art room at the Virginia F. Cartwright Primary School in a fugue state. By the last morning period, she was barely aware of her students at all, despite their enthusiastic, bold interpretations of Van Gogh.

Gail popped her head in at lunch to find Rosie at her desk, mindlessly spooning sugar-free yogurt into her mouth while she checked the art show flyer for typos.

"So, when's the big date?" When Rosie only blinked at her, Gail continued on. "You look like an under-rested owl. When are you meeting Tom?"

Rosie stared into her yogurt. "I'm not."

"What do you mean, you're not? Rosie—"

"I told you the rest of the story. You know how improbable the whole thing is. Connecting over maple syrup? Both of us widowed?" She abandoned her lunch, such as it was. "We don't waltz off into the sunset together. That doesn't happen."

Gail braced herself in the doorway. "Maybe it does."

"He's got kids."

"I'm guessing they're not babies."

"He lives in Boston."

"It's four hours with a stop to pee."

"Gail." Rosie's head ached. "It's ridiculous."

"So you're just going to let him go home?" Gail's voice crescendoed. "Rosie."

Rosie let her silence speak for itself.

Gail drew in air enough to howl down the entire specials corridor, but she released the doorframe and pulled the door shut behind her as she entered, pushing the breath out in a huff. "How long have we been teaching together?"

Rosie sighed. "Twenty years?"

"Nineteen." Gail corrected her. "The first year I was here, I was all on my own. Marty was deployed, three months from his discharge, and I was scared to death. New job, no friends, husband in the line of fire, too broke from relocating to go to my family. And there was you." She pulled out one of the student sized stools and sat across the desk. "You and Tim were living up in Catmint Gap, and you invited me to come to your folks' Christmas dinner in town.

"You shine when you're with your people. I saw that when I walked into the front hall of that big old house. Your parents, all the crazy cousins, Ted and his family. Your scary old Granny Yolie... It was the best kind of chaos."

Rosie couldn't stop the tears that welled up and spilled over at the memory. It had been a spectacular Christmas. The house on

Chapel Street had been full to bursting. Her parents had just moved in with Granny Yolie, there were relatives spilling out of every corner, laughter loud enough to mute her brother's insistence at singing carols by the out-of-tune piano, and so much food.

All gone now. Ted and Camille to Santa Fe. Granny Yolie to old age. Her mother, stolen too young. Tim, taken before she could fully grasp the idea of life without him, and then the disease which stole her father from her long before it took his life. Gradually, they'd all faded away from her, and she'd ended up just like her granny, alone in the Chapel Street house, but without a sweet, handsome son and his charming, beautiful wife to move in and keep an eye on her in her dotage.

No son at all. No daughter.

"Your light dimmed a little when you lost them, but it's not gone. Not as long as you have me, and your students, but Rosie. I saw you glow yesterday. Just glow, and I can't sit here and say nothing while you let that go."

The recess bell rang, saving Rosie from further assault on the decision she already regretted. Gail swept herself out of the room, pausing for one last barrage.

"It's never too late."

The village of Thornton looked like a Norman Rockwell painting, until you noticed the modern cars and road signs. Then the rest of the twenty-first century tells asserted themselves. Tommy stopped to look in the windows of every shop, every café, on the off chance Rosie might be there.

The disappointment of not hearing from her had boiled down to a restless night and a hazy morning. He'd woken up more angry than sad, but that hadn't stopped him from taking the scenic route through the downtown, instead of passing by altogether when the state highway brushed up against the common. He'd parked his car near a diner, watching a group of students cross the road, backpacks and ball caps like a uniform.

They made him miss his own kids, so he texted that he would be home late, and promised to let them know he was home safe. It was a new habit Kayla in particular insisted on since Ellen's death.

At the end of a block of shops the road crossed a river. Tommy read the plaque on the corner of the mill building that squatted adjacent the east side of the bridge.

Memorial Bridge, dedicated in grateful remembrance of those who gave their lives in service of their country
1914-1918

The bridge spanned a waterfall, which sent a fine spray up to reflect what sunlight struggled through the overcast sky. The river rushed over the plunge, pouring noisily over the rocks below, swirling in a scummy whorl before rolling away and around a bend. He recalled Sterling saying something about the north flowing river, and wondered if, wherever she was, Rosie could see it.

"My parents had their first kiss here."

At first, he assumed he was hearing things, but her hand closed over his, softer, warmer than the stone beneath, but no less real. Her cuticles were stained with ink and maybe paint or clay.

Tommy didn't dare look at her. "I wish I knew where my parents' first kiss was. Probably in a movie theatre. My ma loved movies."

"I'm sorry I didn't call. I wasn't to going to come." She looked out over the river. "This is nothing I ever expected."

Tommy turned, taking her hand between his, willing her to look at him. "That's why I can't let it go. I felt something the moment I saw you. We're good together, and…"

"And?"

"I'm too old to ignore something like that." She turned to him, the breeze from the falls whipping her hair into her eyes. He tucked a stray lock behind her ear. "I'd like to come back for a couple of days, maybe spend some time with you. See this town through your eyes."

When she smiled, Tommy felt the light of it in his veins.

"When spring finally gets here, it's just gorgeous."

He leaned in, his lips close to the corner of hers. "It's gorgeous right now."

It was Rosie who shifted to bring her mouth to his. Tommy thought maybe second kisses were underrated, particularly when Rosie leaned into him.

He wrapped an arm around her and whispered, "Some time, I wouldn't mind kissing you someplace less public."

"Mmm. I think that would be nice." She leaned back suddenly. "Where will you stay. I mean, it's not like we need chaperones, but we did just meet two days ago…"

He hugged her, delighted by her line of thinking. "My daughter raves about staying in spare rooms she finds on the internet. In a town like this, I bet I could find a place or two. Or that hotel I drove by on the common?"

"Not there. That house belonged to my mother's parents." With a laugh, Rosie linked her arm with his, and steered him back toward the heart of the village. "My Grandma Fletcher's ghost would haunt you for sure."

Tommy matched his steps to hers. "We'll figure it out."

"My house is too big for just me." She blushed happily. "Whatever happens, Tommy, you're welcome there."

~

ALSO BY CAMERON D. GARRIEPY

Thornton Vermont

Damselfly Inn

Sweet Pease

Family Practice

Sugaring Season: Stories from Thornton & Beyond

Bread & Promises (Yuletide)

The Best Laid Plans: A Socially Distanced Thornton Vermont Romance

Green Mountain Hearts

Ambitious Heart

Unbound Heart

Troubadour Heart

Green Mountain Hearts: the Complete Series (paperback only)

Standalone Romance

Buck's Landing

Short Fiction in Anthologies

Valentine (Metaphysical Gravity)

Requiring of Care (Echoes in Darkness)

Christmas Mini-Romances

Tempests & Temptations: Two Christmas Romances

Bread & Promises (Yuletide)

Cinnamon Girl (Wish/Sugaring Season)

The Soloist (Joy)

Star of Wonder (Merry Little Christmas)

Santa's Photographer (Secret Santas)

Merry's Christmas (Atlantic to Pacific)

Twelve Days 'til Christmas

CHILDREN OF THE PARALLELS

SPECULATIVE MIDDLE GRADE SHORT FICTION

Parallel Jump

Parallel Hunt

ABOUT THE AUTHOR

Cameron D. Garriepy attended a small Vermont college in a town very like Thornton. She's missed it since the day she packed up her Subaru and drove off into the real world. Some might say she created the fictional village as wish fulfillment, and they would be correct.

She is the author of the Thornton Vermont Series, and the founder of Bannerwing Books, a co-op of independent authors. Prior to Bannerwing, Cameron was an editor at Write on Edge, where she edited three volumes of the online writing group's literary anthology, Precipice. Cameron appeared in the inaugural cast of Listen to Your Mother - Boston, and irregularly contributes flash fiction to the Word Count Podcast.

Since her time at Middlebury College, Cameron has worked as a nanny, a pastry cook, and an event ticket resale specialist. In her spare time, she cooks, gardens, knits, reads avidly, and researches hobby farming—chickens and goats are just waiting for her ship to come in. She writes from the greater Boston area, where she lives with her husband, son, and a geriatric pug.

Connect with Cameron online at www.camerondgarriepy.com
Hear first about sales and new releases via Cameron's newsletter—
subscribe at
www.bit.ly/cdgnewsletter
Join the conversation in Cameron's Facebook group at www.
bit.ly/thorntonfbgroup

amazon.com/author/camerondgarriepy

facebook.com/camerondgarriepy

twitter.com/camerongarriepy

goodreads.com/camerondgarriepy

bookbub.com/authors/cameron-d-garriepy

instagram.com/camerongarriepy

pinterest.com/camerongarriepy

ABOUT THE PUBLISHER

Bannerwing Books is a writers' co-op founded in 2012 by Cameron D. Garriepy, and completed by Angela Amman and Mandy Dawson. Currently residing on Slack, somewhere in the ether between Boston, Detroit, and Paso Robles, Bannerwing presents works by Stephanie Ayers, Ericka Clay, and Liz Zimmers, as well as collections featuring Andra Watkins, Kate Shrewsday, and Kameko Murakami.

www.bannerwingbooks.com

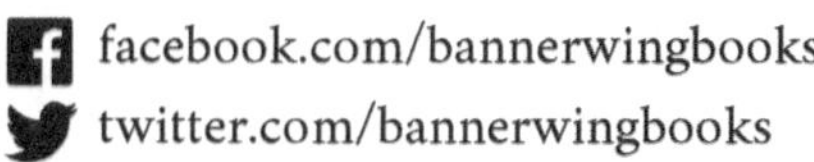

facebook.com/bannerwingbooks
twitter.com/bannerwingbooks